Me and My Hittas 4

Tranay Adams

Me and My Hittas 4

Me and My Hittas 4/ Tranay Adams-1st ed. © 2016

ISBN: 978-1-7377789-8-1

Email: dopereadzpresents@gmail.com

Facebook: Tranay Adams

Instagram: Tranay Adams

Cover Artist: Divine

The atmosphere reeked of blood and sweat. The white tiled floor had been scrubbed with every cleaning product you could name, buffed and waxed, but there were still faint splotches of blood that wouldn't come up. Many fighters had been left quadriplegics, and some had even lost their lives inside of the savage battle arena. But that didn't stop the two gladiators from going at it like a couple of starving wolves over a fresh kill.

Crack!

Whack!

Thrack!

Clayvon delivered a three punch combination to his opponent that made him stagger back. He'd almost fell but righted himself before his bare back could kiss the floor. After regaining control of his equilibrium, the six-four Russian whipped his head back around. He glared at Clayvon, snapped his broken nose back into place, and wiped the blood from his lip with the back of his bandaged fist. He screamed at the top of his lungs and charged at his opponent.

The millionaires and trainers rooted for the fighter that they wanted to win. There were cheers, hoots and hollers coming from the audience as they were egging their respective fighters on. There were hundreds of thousands of dollars and even some million dollars bets that had been laid. You had to have your dollars up to be able to bet in this fighting league. It was a billion dollar business, and only the wealthiest of the wealthy could throw their hats into the pot.

Clayvon bobbed, weaved and ducked the punches, uppercuts, and hooks that his opponent came at him with. He then came up with an uppercut that was reminiscent of the Mortal Kombat video game. It was so powerful that it split the Russian's jaw in half and sent a mist of blood into the air. The foreigner fell on his back with his eyes rolled to their whites and a crimson mouth. He groaned in excruciation as red streams flowed over his chin. Some of the guys in the audience were pissed while others were in frenzy over the win. The referee, who was a short Puerto Rican man, grasped Clayvon's wrist and raised his hand into the air, declaring him the victor in broken Spanish accent.

"It's because of that kid right there that I'm $500,000 dollars richer." Black Jesus lit up an Arturo Fuentes cigar and took a few puffs. "By the time I leave here I'll have a million dollars."

"Yeah, he and Gouch have been putting in that work," Gangsta stated, keeping his eyes on the youngster with the frizzy cornrows. "I'm sitting on two-hundred and fifty kay 'cause of them." He looked across the way to Gouch. He had a towel draped over his head, and Shelly was behind him massaging his shoulders. Gouch gave him a slight smirk and winked at him; Gangsta gave him a nod. He then leaned over and whispered into Killa Dre's ear. The young nigga walked backwards until he was swallowed by the audience. One minute later, he emerged on the end of the room where Gouch and Shelly was. He was standing behind Shelly, but he was oblivious to his presence.

The fights went on with body after body crashing onto the floor. Some of the fighters left the arena crippled for life, others left in body bags and the lucky ones left with minor injuries. At the end of the night only two fighters were left to take the floor. Gouch found himself pitted against Clayvon; a man who had ran through his opponents with little difficulty just as he did. Gouch had fought many men in his twenty-seven years on earth, and he'd beaten them all. But somehow he wasn't so sure of himself when it came to his younger opponent. For the first time since he was six years old, and had his first fight, he had butterflies in his stomach.

Gouch bounced from his left leg to his right, bending his neck from left to right. Clayvon's one good eye was dead locked on him; sweat ran over his brow and trickled off of it. He cracked his knuckles but never broke eye contact with his competition.

Kenny Masters stood at the center of both men with a microphone in his hand. He looked between the two fighters, smiling as he brought the microphone to his lips. "Here we are y'all the tournament has been narrowed down to these two fighters. To my right I have, Clayvon 'The Hit-man' Coles," the audience went wild with cheers, "and to my left I have, Gouch 'Crazy Hands' Hood." the audience went wild with cheers again. "This is it my niggaz. The Rumble in the Jungle,

The Brawl for it All, the fight that will determine which one of these mothafuckaz will be leaving here with one million dollars in cold, hard cash." He said in a game show host type of voice. He lifted his arm high, and brought it down saying, "Kick ass!"

Ding!

Ding!

Ding!

The bell sounded, lighting fuses in both Gouch and Clayvon. They charged each other, full speed ahead. Nearing one another, they leap into the air and swinging their feet at one another's heads. Their legs connect, duplicating a sound reminiscent of a bamboo stick striking a bamboo tree. The fighters landed to their feet and were quickly back at it, going punch for punch and kick for kick. Clayvon laid into Gouch throwing haymakers for his face and head. Gouch brought his arms up, allowing his arms to absorb the assault. Although none of his opponent's power punches connected, he could feel the bones of his arms throbbing and aching.

Clayvon faked like he was about to throw another haymaker and kicked him on the side of his knee. The searing pain caused Gouch to grimace and drop his guard, leaving his head open for attack. Clayvon swung his steel-toe booted foot around and slammed it into the side of his dome. Seeing himself about to hit the floor, Gouch used his hand to catch himself and brought his feet across Clayvon's face, one foot at a time. The attack made the younger man stumble backwards, but he quickly caught his self. Gouch rushed him again, unleashing a flurry of punches into his torso.

"That's right, get'em!" Shelly egged Gouch on. "Kick his mothafucking ass!"

Crack!

Crack!

Thrack!

Brack!

Gouch stumbled back from the devastating blows, but caught himself, massaging his jaw. Standing erect, he listened to the chants of the audience as they egg him and Clayvon on.

The eye-patch rocking fighter walked toward his opponent calmly as if he was strolling through the park.

"Fuck are you doing? Kick his ass!" Shelly barked on Gouch.

"No." Gouch told him.

"What? We had a deal!" Shelly looked at him like he was crazy. He was so close to that million dollars that he could smell it, and here Gouch was about to piss it away.

"Fuck that deal, Blood!"

"You black, bug eyed, burnt face bitch!" Shelly hurled his insults. "I'ma blow your monkey ass up!" Spittle flew from his lips. He was so mad that he couldn't pull the detonator from his pocket fast enough. It snagged on the inside pocket, but he eventually pulled it free. Gouch gave a nod to someone hidden in the audience, just as Shelly was clearing the detonator out of his pocket. The old man's eyes bugged, his nose flared, and his mouth opened as wide as it could as he released a bloodcurdling scream. Killa Dre pulled his switchblade from out of Shelly's calf muscle and wiped it off on his handkerchief.

Seeing the window of opportunity open, Gouch kicked the detonator loose from Shelly's hand. The detonator flew up into the air and he kicked it in Gangsta's direction. Gangsta caught the detonator and smashed it against the handle of Black Jesus' wheelchair until it crumbled into pieces, like a stale cookie.

"No!" Shelly bellowed. He leapt forth and cracked Gouch in the jaw, dropping him. He ran as fast as he could with one good leg toward one of the security guards. The security guard made to shoot him, but his fists were like lighting as they tore into him. He punched him twice in the torso, kneed him and chopped him at the back of his neck. The man howled in pain and crumpled to the floor. Shelly picked up his assault rifle and spun around, spitting rapid fire and laying the other security guards down. The chatter of the weapon caused the audience to scramble and duck for cover, even Kenny Masters was getting the fuck out of dodge. After laying the security guards down, a very pissed off Shelly whipped his weapon around to Gouch. Gouch had just stood to his feet when a single round fled from the barrel of the AK-47.

Everything seemed to be moving in slow motion as the missile shaped bullet soared in his direction, rotating counter clockwise.

"Ughhh," Clayvon came out of nowhere tackling Gouch to the floor, narrowly missing the bullet. They hit the linoleum with a thud. Shelly went to fire the AK-47 again and it clicked empty. Seeing Gangsta, Killa Dre, Kenny Masters and Gouch coming after him, the old man tossed the assault rifle aside and made a mad dash toward the door. He threw all of his weight at the locks of the double doors and one of the doors came crashing to the porch. He scrambled to his feet and limped as fast as he could toward his rental. Killa Dre was the first out of the door, followed by Kenny Masters gripping one of the dead security guard's assault rifles.

"Mothafucka, come into my house and fuck my shit up? Unh uh!" Kenny Masters took aim with his assault rifle. Killa Dre came to his side after snatching his gun from off the back tire of the limousine. He pointed his weapon at the fleeing car along with Kenny Masters. They dumped on the car at the same time, shattering its back window and blowing out its back lights. Once they could no longer see the back of the car, they ceased fire and lowered their weapons to their sides. Gouch, Gangsta, Clayvon and Brutus came hurrying down the steps.

"Y'all get'em?" Gouch inquired.

"Naw, mothafucka got away, Blood." Killa Dre said, tucking his tool on his waistline.

"I know where he's going." Gouch informed them.

"Well, let's go. Come on." Gangsta ran back into the mansion to get Black Jesus.

Gouch turned around to Clayvon. "Thanks, man."

"You're welcome." Clayvon shook his hand firmly. "You know you owe me a rematch."

"You got it. If you were pulling those punches I'd hate to see what I'm in store for. But I'll be looking forward to the challenge, though."

The limousine blew its horn.

Gangsta stuck his head out of the back window and waved him on, saying, "Come on, Gucci!"

"Gotta go," Gouch ran off.

Kenny Masters and Clayvon watched the backlights of the limousine until they disappeared into the night. Someone clearing their throat at Kenny's rear gave him cause to turn around.

"Homeboy forfeited, so that million is ours." Brutus said. "I'd like to collect."

Kenny Masters nodded his head and said, "Let me have my guys get rid of these bodies and I'll pay everyone. Come on." He motioned for them to follow him with his assault rifle as he headed for the steps.

$$$

Shelly limped down into the basement as fast as he could, panting out of breath. His dogs rushed to him barking and jumping upon his pants legs, happy to see him. "Not now fellas, daddy's gotta boogie." He grabbed a suitcase that was buried underneath a pile of clothes. He slung it upon the bed and began throwing clothes into it by the handful. He threw a few other things on top of the clothes that he felt was valuable to him. He closed the suitcase, which now had shirt sleeves and pants legs hanging out of it, and grabbed it from out of the bed. He smacked his lucky Dodgers cap upon his head and grabbed his trusty stick. "Come on fellas." He motioned for his dogs to follow him with his stick.

Shelly and his dogs were heading for the door when they heard the basement door being kicked open. The door bounced off of the wall and a stampede of footsteps could be heard hurrying down the steps. Shelly threw down his suitcase and stick. He went to grab the gun from the front of his jeans, but then he realized that he hadn't tucked it. With that in mind, he ran to the place where he stashed his banger, leaving his dogs growling and barking at the doorway.

Shelly had just lifted his mattress and grabbed his Glock when Gouch, Gangsta and Killa Dre came rushing into his doorway. Gouch was lifting his banger to point it at the old man when he was whipping around to take a shot at him. Their fingers curled around the triggers of their weapons at the exact same time.

Bloc!

Boc!

Shelly's bullet whizzed by Gouch's head and crashed into the edge of the doorway. The shot that Gouch got off landed right in that bitch ass nigga'z chest cavity. Gritting his teeth, he fell back onto the floor and dropped his gun. Gouch stepped to him with his gun leveled at his chest, kicking his burner aside. The banger spun flew across the floor spinning around in circles before wedging its self underneath an old refrigerator.

"Ouch! You fucking shot me!" Shelly hollered out, looking to a hand of blood having touched his wound.

"Killa, whack this old nigga'z dogs, Blood. I'ma tuck him in." Gouch spoke to the young nigga, but kept his eyes on his victim.

Shelly crawled over to Gouch and wrapped his arms around his leg, pleading. "Oh, please, please, don't kill my dogs, man. They're all I got." He stared up at him with teary eyes, looking like a sad ass puppy.

"Nigga, you worried about them punk ass dogs' lives when you need to be worried about your own." Gouch looked down upon a sobbing Shelly. The mothafucka was pitiful. It amazed him how a man that had been so arrogant and confident two hours ago, had been reduced to groveling behind a couple of mangy mutts. Gouch made a mental note to never love something so much that it would have him in the same position that the poor bastard at his feet was in.

"Man, fuck all of that." Gouch yanked his leg back from Shelly and brought his burner into play. "See ya, I wouldn't wanna be ya." He gave the nigga his parting words before letting that thang go in his face. Each pull of his trigger made it sound like thunder erupting down in the basement. The last sounds besides the dogs barking were the empty shell casings dancing on the floor. Once Gouch finished the deed, he lowered his smoking gun at his side and studied his handiwork.

"Dre." He called out to his little homie.

"What's up with it?"

"Take care of them mutts."

The dogs barking grew louder and louder. They were heated as a mothafucka having seen their master slain. Just seconds after Gouch gave the order it was executed.

Boc! Boc! Boc! Boc!

"Let's roll." Gouch motioned for Killa Dre with his gun as he headed for the door.

Everyday above ground was a good day.

Chapter one

Meanwhile

Monk sat on a stool at the kitchen counter playing solitary with his self. A black .44 Magnum revolver rested on his waistline as if he had a license to carry. He involuntarily tapped his foot and chewed on a straw from a Big Gulp he'd gotten earlier in the night. About twenty minutes ago he'd gotten a call from a couple of chicks that claimed they'd successfully killed Paybacc and were now looking to collect the bounty on his head. At first he thought they were bullshitting, but then they texted him a picture of Paybacc with a bullet hole in his forehead. He was for sure he was dead now, and was even more impressed that a couple of broads had put in the work. He reasoned that times were hard with the recession and people were willing to do whatever they had to in order to make a buck. He gave the girls the address where they were to meet him with Paybacc's body for confirmation and payment of the bounty.

Monk put down his cards and picked up his bottle of Budweiser, taking it to the head. He sat the bottle down on the counter and wiped his mouth with the back of his hand. He glanced at the Timex watch that adorned his wrist, and for the hundredth time, peeked under the flap of the bag that held the $50,000 dollars that was the bounty on Paybacc's head. He closed the flap and went back to his game of solitary.

"Ah, fuck!" Playboy cursed after losing a game in Madden. He was a slim dude who rocked a shadow fade that swirled with waves. He wore glasses, not because his sight was bad, but for fashion. Princess cut diamond earrings hung from his lobes, twinkling under the soft light of the living room. His fit was a Louie Vuitton button-down with silver cufflinks and matching loafers. He was a pretty boy that lived for fast money, fast cars, and even faster women.

"You tryna run that shit back?" Banga asked.

"Yeah, run that shit back, dawg."

"Alright, I'ma 'bout to chip your old fiddle ass again," Banga sat up on the couch.

He was a chubby dude that had just enough hair around his mouth to be called a goatee. He wore an Oakland Raiders beanie and a matching sweatshirt. He sported his socks pulled up to his knees and had black All-Star Chuck Taylor Converse on his feet. A cigarette rested between his chubby fingers as he worked the joystick of the PS4, dropping ashes.

Banga and Playboy was a couple of young brothers from the set. They had a knack for putting in work and had a drive for getting paper that was unheard of. This made them Killa Dre's pick of the litter to have on the team. All of the time he'd spent around Pavielle had come in handy. Not only did Killa Dre have a knack for hustling, he also had an eye for picking talent. He'd heard enough about the brothers to know they'd be a valuable asset to the team, which is why he didn't waste time recruiting them into the fold.

"Yo, Monk, that bag of Loud over there by you, bruh?" Banga asked. His eyes were focused on the screen, but he was talking to the older G.

"Yeah, it's over here." Monk replied, seeing the ounce of Kush on the counter.

"Do me a favor, O.G. I got some Cigarillos over here, twist one up for me."

Monk put his cards down and turned around on the stool. "Young nigga, I got one goddamn hand, how in the fuck am I 'pose to roll you a blunt?"

Banga and Playboy busted up laughing.

"My bad, G, I forgot you were handicap and shit." Banga said.

A car honking outside drew Monk's attention to the window. He took a peek through the curtains and saw a white Celebrity idling inside the alley. He let the curtain fall and turned around to the twins.

"Who that, Monk?" Playboy asked over his shoulder.

"It's them bitches that's 'pose to drop homeboy's body off to us." Monk informed him. "Y'all come outside with me. If this is some funny shit, lay them hoes out."

Banga and Playboy put on their game-faces. They picked their burners up from the coffee-tPlayboy and tucked them into their waistlines. They followed behind Monk as he headed into the kitchen for the back porch door.

$$$

Playboy unlocked the padlock and removed the chain from around the gate. He pulled the gate back and allowed the Celebrity to roll inside. The raggedy vehicle slowly coasted over the threshold. The first thing Monk noticed about the car was its busted headlight and knocking engine. It was a wonder to him how the old heap was still running, and more importantly, why its driver would risk using it to transport a dead body when there was a great possibility that it could break down or get pulled over by the police.

As the Celebrity pulled upon the backyard lawn and executed its engine, Banga and Playboy joined Monk by his side. They watched as the doors of the hoopty swung open and two women stepped into view. The first was a slim chick who rocked her hair in burgundy cornrows. The second was a thick, chocolate sister with full lips. Both of the women were draped in black from head to toe. They wore hard faces as they stepped around to the trunk of the Celebrity.

"What's up?" Burgundy cornrows said in greeting, throwing her head back.

"'Sup? What you got for me?" Monk asked.

"You got our money?" Thick interjected.

"It isn't your money yet, at least not until I view the merchandise." Monk stated firmly.

"Alright, nigga, we're gonna pop this trunk, but y'all bet not try to fuck us." Thick balled her face.

"Ain't nobody gone try to fuck you. All we tryna do is see if y'all really killed this nigga or not." Banga added his two cents. His scowling made him look like a young Ice Cube in his N.W.A days.

"Right," Playboy chimed in. "It's kind of hard to believe King Crab is dead, especially with all of the stories we've heard about him. Niggaz will have you believing he's the Jason Voorhees of gangbanging, like you can try to kill'em but he just won't die, feel me?"

"Ain't nobody tryna fuck y'all." Monk told them. "If y'all really got'em in the trunk like y'all said y'all did, then I'll be fifty bands short of being broke. All I want is confirmation. After that y'all can get y'all paper and be gone."

Cornrows looked to thick and she gave a nod. Cornrows motioned Monk over as she went to open the trunk of the Celebrity. She lifted the trunk and exposed something wrapped up in black trash bags. She leaned over into the trunk and ripped open the trash bag, revealing Paybacc's solemn face. Smiles emerged on Banga and Playboy's faces and they gave one another a pound.

While Banga and Playboy were busy celebrating, Monk was studying Paybacc's face. He noticed something really peculiar about him but he couldn't quite put his finger on it. His forehead crinkled when it dawned on him what wasn't right. That's when he looked to cornrows and said, "I thought y'all shot this nigga in the head."

At that precise moment, Paybacc's eyes popped open and he swung his Calico around, cracking off two shots. Monk's face twisted into agony and he fell to the ground, bleeding like a stuck pig. Playboy went for burner on his waistline and Traquila shot him his bellie; he screamed aloud and fell into a heap. Banga was right behind his brother reaching for his waistline. He'd already drawn his piece and sent a hot-one through Traquila's throat. Dropping her weapon, she clutched the blood squirting wound in her neck and hit the dirt, grimacing.

"Mothafucka," Passion cried out, her eyes welling with tears. She pumped two through Banga's belly; the slugs ignited a blazing fire inside of him upon entree. Before his back hit the dirt Passion was en route to her best-friend and lover. She stopped short to deposit two slugs into a groaning Playboy's heart before dropping to her knees and scooping Traquila into her arms. She sobbed as she watched her friend gurgle up blood and spill it from the sides of her mouth. She stared up into Passion's eyes as she fought for her life, tooth and nail. Once Traquila grew still, Passion closed her eyes with a brush of her hand and kissed her tenderly on the forehead.

"Who else is in the house?" Paybacc asked Monk as he held a sneaker to his heaving chest. His menacing eyes bored down into his face as he clenched his jaws tightly, nostrils flaring.

"Go fuck yourself!" Monk spat between winces, his one good hand holding onto his enemy's leg.

"The house is clear!" Domino said from the back porch where he stood beside Wacko, both of them donning ski-masks and holding assault rifles. They'd kicked in the front door and stormed in as soon as the first shot was fired. They were going to execute anyone else who may be inside the house before they could act as reinforcements for Monk and them.

"We found the dough, too." Wacko held up the bag containing the fifty bands of cash.

Domino pulled off his ski-mask and stepped off of the back porch. He looked passed Paybacc and saw Passion holding a lifeless Traquila in her arms. His face soured staring at the sight before him and he shook his head. "Damn. They got Tra." he said to himself crossing his heart in the name of the Lord.

"Yeah," Paybaccc sighed and crossed his heart in the sign as well. "Watch her for me; I got something I have to attend to."

"Okilla," Domino nodded.

Paybacc grabbed Monk by the back of his shirt and pulled him up the steps of the back porch into the house. He smacked all of the items from off of the kitchen table and hoisted Monk's body upon it. Next, he searched the kitchen until he found what he was looking for: a meat cleaver. He sat it on his intended victim's stomach and tore off the sleeve of his shirt. Afterwards, he balled the sleeve up and stuffed it into Monk's mouth, gagging him. He then picked up the meat cleaver and flipped it over in his palm.

"I'm not even gonna bother asking you where Gangsta is 'cause I already know what you're gonna tell me. But what I am gonna do is, finish the job that I started ten years ago." Paybacc held Monk's last good arm down and struck it with the meat cleaver, with all of his might. Monk tried to scream, but the gag muffled the sound. Paybacc continued to hack away at the arm, and with each strike his victim's eyes rolled further to the back of his head. Monk eventually went into shock, shaking slightly on the table top. Seeing that his arm was holding on to what little bone was left, Paybacc worked it back and forth until it eventually snapped off. He casted the severed arm aside and took the man's right-leg. He lifted the meat cleaver above his head and brought it down.

Thrack!

An hour later

"Oh God, no, fuck me! Fuck me!" Gangsta cursed, pounding the wall with the hand that held his chrome .45. He leaned his forehead against the wall for a moment, breathing heavily. He then looked back at the kitchen table Monk's bloody torso was on. He closed his eyes and shook his head, hating to see what was done to his friend. Looking up, he saw open spelled out in blood across the cupboard above the stove.

Gangsta opened the cupboard, and when he saw Monk's severed head he nearly lost his dinner. He tucked his .45 on his waistline and picked up his friend's head. Sitting it on the table top, he noticed that Monk's eyes were rolled to their corners and his tongue peeked out the side of his mouth. Upon further inspection, he also noticed that there was something stuffed in Monk's mouth. He fished around in Monk's mouth and produced a folded piece of paper. He unfolded the piece of paper and You're next was written on it. Gangsta balled up the piece of paper and threw it aside.

Gouch stepped into the house carrying his gun at his side. "Yo, man, Playboy is dead, but Banga is still…" the words died in his throat when he stumbled upon Monk's bloody torso. The sight was grotesque and reminded him of something he once saw in a horror movie. Gouch hung his head and massage the bridge of his nose. He then looked up and asked, "Who did this, unc? Who you catch a beef with?"

"Paybacc," Gangsta answered.

"Who the fuck is Paybacc?" Gouch's forehead wrinkled.

"A loose end I should have tied up a long time ago." Gangsta admitted. He felt that it was all of his fault that his homeboys had gotten slaughtered like they had.

Chapter Two

Domino cupped his hands under the running faucet and splashed water on his face. He turned the faucet off and took a good look at his reflection in the medicine cabinet mirror. He closed his eyes and let the water drip off of his face. Images of Paybacc chopping off Monk's legs and arm flashed behind his eyelids. He could hear the muffled screams of the man in his head, along with the sound of the meat cleaver hitting his warm flesh. He then saw Monk's severed head with its eyes staring out of their corners and its tongue peeking out the side of its mouth. Suddenly, the head's eyes looked to him at the same time someone was knocking at the door, startling him. He heard the door creep open and turned around, reaching for the banger on his waistline. He let his hand fall to his side once he saw that it was Wacko.

"You all right, foolie?" Wacko asked concerned.

Domino nodded and replied, "I'm one hunnit, cuz."

"Well, we out here. Paybacc is waiting for you so he can divide up that paper."

Domino and Wacko came back into the living room. Passion was sitting on the couch with swollen bloodshot eyes, staring aimlessly. She looked like she was about to crack up at any minute, if she hadn't already. Domino and Wacko pulled up a chair at the table where Paybacc was already seated. Scattered on the table was a handgun, two blocks of cocaine and a few bands of dead presidents. All of which were recovered once they rushed up in Gangsta's trap and twisted a few fools.

"Alright, we gotta hunnit and twenty bands and two bricks of raw." Paybacc announced. "I'ma split the dough up three ways, y'all can have that. I'm taking the bricks, though. I can put it into rotation with the rest of the shit. Is there anyone that objects to that?"

"Nah, it's cool." Domino replied.

"Fine by me," Wacko answered.

"Passion?" Paybacc called her.

"Alright," She agreed, wiping her tearing eyes with her fingers.

Paybacc swept forty grand each into three paper shopping bags. He used an extra bag to place the two blocks of cocaine into and set it aside. Next, he picked up one of the bags and held it out toward Passion.

"Passion," Paybacc called for her. She approached him and took the bag. She leaned forth and kissed his lips. "Call me when you get home." He told her as she pulled open the front door. Once she was gone, he handed Domino and Wacko their individual bags of money.

"Yo, fam, I think you should let me follow old girl home and put her outta her misery." Wacko said seriously, placing the bag between his legs. "You see how fucked up she is behind homegirl getting peeled? She'll end up going on a guilt trip and spilling her guts to them boys. I don't know about chu, but I aint even tryna have that happen. I'm allergic to prison."

"Nigga, you ain't never been." Domino frowned.

"That's right. Ain't never been and ain't ever tryna go, feel me?"

"Nah, she won't say anything." Paybacc assured him.

"How you figure?" Wacko twisted his lips and angled his head.

"'Cause she's dicknotized, fool." Paybacc told him. "She already confessed her undying love for me. Why you think she agreed to go on this lil' caper? Bitch loves me."

"I'm not one to gamble on another man's dick." Wacko stated. "You can put your faith in your swipe if you want to, but I prefer putting my faith in one of these," he patted the gun that was bulging underneath his shirt, "its wayyyyy more reliable."

"Like I said, no one is to touch lil' momma until I say otherwise." Paybacc stated sternly, looking Wacko dead in his eyes.

Wacko put his hands together and thought on it. "Let's say I sleep walk, and I just so happen to take a drive over to her apartment, I make my way inside into her bedroom and my gun just so happens to go off? What if that was to happen? That's hypothetically speaking, of course."

"Well," Paybacc took his time lighting a cigarette and then blew smoke. "I'll take a lil' drive out to Pasadena, you know? To that retirement home that your grandmother stays at; I'll creep into her room and hide in the closet and right when she comes back from recreation, I'll slip a length of wire around her neck and then I'll tighten it until the old bitch dies. Oh, and that's not hypothetically speaking. That's exactly what the fuck is gone happen should any harm come to my bitch, lil' nigga!" he threatened, spittle flying from off of his lips.

Wacko scowled and his face twitched with anger. Paybacc hit a soft spot when he threatened the life of his grandmother. She'd cared for him since he was a kid and had been a surrogate mother to him. Wacko pulled the banger from off his hip and pointed it at Paybacc's smug expression. The O.G went about his business of smoking his cigarette as if he didn't have a care in the world.

Domino looked between his mentor and his protégé. He wore a shocked expression. He couldn't believe the scene that was playing out before his eyes. "Yo, what the fuck are you two niggaz doing, man? We all homies, the enemy is out there." He threw his head toward the door. "Our guns are supposed to be going off on them, not on each other. Wacko, I told you once before this man is like my father, and you're like my lil' bro. What the fuck, man. Y'all are my family." He clutched his head trying to make sense of the madness.

Wacko sat on the opposite end of the table with his banger pointed in Paybacc's direction. His face was like a mad dog foaming at the mouth, but quickly softened to a childlike smile and laugh. "I'm just fucking with the big homie, cuz. You know it's all love over this way." He assured Domino.

"I gotta go." Paybacc said, grabbing his bag of bricks. "I'll get up witchu niggaz later." He slapped hands with Domino and Wacko before taking his leave.

"Wack, what the fuck was that? You was 'bout to blast the homie." Domino asked once Paybacc had left. He was staring at the little nigga like he'd lost his goddamn mind.

"Was? I still am." Wacko said seriously. "Nigga gone threaten my grand momma life over some ratchet, fuck he think I am? I'ma finish what Gangsta should have long ago, that's on the gang. But first, I'ma get whatever he got stashed in that chest."

"We've already been over this, cuz. We're not robbing him." Domino put his foot down.

"You don't wanna rob the nigga, and you don't wanna kill the nigga." Wacko said annoyed. "Well, what the fuck do you want to do then?"

"We're not robbing him, and that's final." Domino spat irritated. Homeboy was getting on his last fucking nerve.

"You're my nigga, and I love you like cooked food, but the friends of my enemies become my enemies." Wacko glared at him and squared his jaws. "So when I walk out that door, I guess I'll have to be looking over my shoulders for two of mine instead of one."

Domino bit down on his bottom lip and nodded his head. "Alright, if you want cuz gone then fuck it, but let's wait until he re-up so we can have something to bubble with."

"Fair enough," Wacko smiled and slapped hands with his nigga. "You had me going for a minute, cuz. I thought I was gone have to zip up both of y'all niggaz."

"Nah, you don't ever have to question my loyalty…ever." Domino swore.

Chapter Three

Gouch road on the passenger side of Gangsta's GT Bentley smoking a cigarette and listening attentively, as his uncle brought him up to speed on everything that occurred in his absence.

"All of this shit happened over a few months span?" Gouch shook his head and felt the burn wounds on the side of his face, "It didn't take long for Booby's lil' reign to go from sugar to shit. Did it?"

"No, it didn't." Gangsta agreed. He watched Gouch feel on his burn wounds on and off again during their conversation, and it became evident to him that he had a complex about it. "Gucci, you know there are surgeons that could probably do something about that. You know my papers long and I got connections. I could see to it that you have the best of doctors to take care of you."

Gouch nodded and said, "I'll have to take a rain check. First things first, we gotta get this nigga Paybacc out of our hair. This nigga bring more drama than four baby mommas."

"On sitas," Gangsta agreed, saying mommas in Spanish.

"You know them fools Arsenegger and Ortiz was there the night the Mexicans raided us and laid the homies down, right?"

"For real?"

Gouch nodded and continued, "I was barely conscious, but I could hear every-

thing…" he began to recount what happened that night when the Mexicans raided the trap, and Arsenegger and Ortiz came in.

Flashback

"You mothafuckaz came here on your feet, but you're leaving in body bags!" Gouch yelled from the top step, clutching his shotgun as it wafted with smoke. "You mothafucking Wet Backs done broke into the wrong nigga'z house!"

Shaved head and Chucky crept to the steps cautiously. Shaved head tried to take a peek up the staircase and Gouch nearly blew his mothafucking head off. He brushed his hand down his stubble head to feel for blood, eyes wide thinking that he had been hit. He was good though. While Gouch talked shit from the top step, shaved head signaled for Chucky to hand him something. The Vato reached inside his overcoat and produced a throwing grenade, passing it off to his comrade. Shaved head pulled the pin, waited a moment, and then threw that bitch up stairs.

Oh, shit!" the eses heard their enemy shout.

Kaboom!

Gouch came tumbling down the stairs a bloody mess, the left side of his face was fried and his eye had discoloration. Chucky spat on his face and kicked him viciously.

"Come on. Let's get the fuck outta here," shaved head nudged Chucky. He heard the police car sirens wailing in the distance. He turned to head for the door and his forehead exploded, bullet flying out the back of his dome. Blood hit the wall behind him and he crumpled to the carpet. Chucky whipped around to start dumping and some hot shit went through his right-eye, exiting out the left side of his skull. He

dropped to his knees and fell over shaved head's body. Together their forms created a bloody heap on the floor.

Arsenegger had both his hands wrapped around Ridah Man's hand, which was holding his smoking .45 automatic handgun. "Alright, you can come out now." he called toward the kitchen. Ortiz emerged from the kitchen with two shopping bags: one had bricks of cocaine and the other had $150,000 dollars in it. The plan was to make the murder scene look like a drug deal gone bad.

Ortiz put one bag in Chucky's hand and the other bag in shaved head's hand. He looked to the corner and saw Chewy on the floor, holding his crotch. His eyes were staring out of their corners and his mouth was ajar. He was dead.

"Poor bastard," Ortiz shook his head sadly as he crossed his heart in the sign of the crucifix.

Arsenegger looked over the bodies scattered on the floor. "Where the fuck is he?" his forehead wrinkled with wonderment.

"Who?" Ortiz raised an eyebrow.

"Booby?"

"He's not here." He looked over the faces of the bodies.

"I'm going to check up stairs, you check down here." Arsenegger pulled his gun from its holster and ascended up the steps strategically.

Ortiz checked the living room, the kitchen, and then took a peek through the curtain. There were about four police cars on the lawn. Arsenegger raced down the steps shoving his weapon back into its holster. "Son of a bitch isn't here! Any luck?"

He shook his head no and said, "All clear down here!"

"It's okay. We'll get him, and all the rest of them, too." Arsenegger assured his partner, touching fists with him. He had a dead serious ass expression on his face.

Detectives Maza and Dupri came through the door, guns drawn, flanked by half a dozen police officers. Maza and the rest of the police holstered their firearms once they spotted the necklace badges around Arsenegger and Ortiz's necks. Maza gave Arsenegger a nod and a wink and he returned the gesture.

"Uh, partner," Ortiz called for Arsenegger.

"Yeah," Arsenegger answered turning around.

"Someone decided to crash another party." He told him, nodding to the space where Gouch's body once was.

Present

"Arsenegger and Ortiz will come gunning for us, unc. There is no doubt in my mind about that." Gouch assured him. "That's why we can't botch this plan."

"It won't get botched." Gangsta gripped his shoulder. "Trust me."

"What's up with Killa?"

"Lil' homie is at the 'spital with Banga, I told him that I'd be by once we finished up our lil' meeting over here."

"I wanna go see my lil' brotha, man, I ain't seen Booby in a minute." Gouch stated. "I wanna see how he's doing."

"We'll get around to it soon, real soon." Gangsta nodded and glanced at his nephew. "But we gotta get rid of these crooked ass Detectives first. As long as they're alive we gotta keep looking over our shoulders. More so with them than

Paybacc 'cause we don't know what the fuck to expect with them."

Once he was buzzed in, Gangsta coasted his whip through the golden gates of Black Jesus' estate and up the path until he reached his home. He parked in the horse shoe driveway and he and Gouch hopped out. They made their way up the two flights of steps that lead to the door of the drug lord's home. Gangsta knocked on the door with the brass knocker, a moment later a sexy Cuban woman answered the door wearing a bright smile. This was the maid, Marisol. Slung over her shoulder was an Uzi .9mm, which she held upon her shoulder as if it were the strap of a backpack.

"Hello, senor Gangsta and senor Gouch." She nodded with a smile. Behind those pearly whites lurked a killer that would catch a body just as fast as she would sweep a floor.

"Hey, Marisol," Gangsta stepped through the door.

"What's up, love?" Gouch came in behind his uncle.

"Mr. Arturo is in the dining room." Marisol informed them.

"Thanks," Gangsta said over his shoulder.

Entering the dining room, Gangsta and Gouch saw Black Jesus sitting at the table with a husky Mexican man wearing a cheap Pearl Wrinkle blue suit and skinny black tie. He rocked slicked back hair and a thick mustache that curled over his top lip.

"You didn't tell me you had company." Gangsta addressed Black Jesus.

"It's alright." The drug lord motioned the uncle and nephew over. He introduced them to the man at the table. The man rose to his feet. When he went to shake Gangsta's hand Gouch got a glimpse of the shield attached to his belt.

"Yo, this mothafucka a detective," Gouch frowned, head snapping from his uncle to the Mexican man sporting the badge.

Gangsta saw the shield on the Mexican man's belt and turned to Black Jesus. "Fuck is this, Jesus? This cat is a detective, man."

"He's alright, trust me. Have a seat." Black Jesus motioned to the chairs. Gangsta blew hard and sat at the table, followed by Gouch who was reluctant. The law being in his presence made him skeptical. "You wanna eliminate Detectives Arsenegger and Ortiz, right? Well, Detective De La Rosa is just the man you need to get you close enough to guarantee it's done."

Detective Ricardo De La Rosa was Black Jesus' mole inside of the Newton Division police department. He was the same man that had handed over the personnel files of Detectives Arsenegger and Ortiz when Creeper had suspected that the twosome had unjustly murdered his younger brother.

"There's a big Poker game coming up that about five other detectives are going to." Detective De La Rosa began. "Now all of these guys are as dirty as they come. I'm talking about a couple of realllll scum bags here."

"Which explains why you're invited?" Gangsta asked.

"Aye, I do what I do to keep a roof over my family's heads and hot meals on the table. I've never gone outside the law to put someone away, or used deadly force when it wasn't warranted. You wanna see a good cop? Well, I'm about as close as you're gonna get to one, pal. Some of the characters inside the department are just as shady as the ones in the streets, but I'm sure I don't have to tell you that." He adjusted his belt and repositioned himself in the chair, glaring at Gangsta like he wanted to punch him in the face.

"Ricardo, please go on." Black Jesus urged him with the sway of his hand.

"Like I was saying, these guys are dirty, real scum bags. Every week they have a Poker night at this Detective's house by the name of Dupri. Well, Dupri and I have been quite friendly with one another so he's invited me to the game. I figure I'll bring in The Gift and a couple of hours into the game I'll make up some bullshit about going to get some more cash from the ATM. I'll wait until I get from off the block; press the little button, like so, and presto. Your problem is up in smoke."

"What about the other cats? You don't feel anything leaving them aboard a sinking ship?" Gangsta inquired.

"Fuck'em!" De La Rosa spat like it was nothing. "They're just as grimy as Arsenegger and Ortiz, maybe even grimier. So don't chu go boohooing over their spilt blood." He took a sip of champagne.

"Oh, you don't have to worry about that." Gangsta assured.

"What do you think?" Black Jesus asked.

"Sounds good."

"So it's a go?"

"It's a go." Gangsta shook hands with Black Jesus and De La Rosa.

$$$

Killa Dre stepped into the doorway of Banga's room. He watched his friend's chest rise and fall as he breathed. He listened as the machines he was hooked up to played their own orchestra. He was sure there had been many men, women, and children that had heard this same chilling musical before they were carried over to the next life by the cold hands of Death. He wondered what went through their minds in their last hours: were they scared, or did they embrace it and go willingly? He didn't know when his time would come, but he knew it could be sooner than most, especially with the life he was leading. He told himself right then and there that when

Death came for him that he would look it right in the eyes and accept his fate, like the G he was.

Killa Dre took a deep breath and approached Banga's bed. As he stood looking over him, his eyes began to flutter and his lips slightly parted as if he was trying to say something.

"What's...what's up, Blood?" Banga croaked.

"Ain't shit, my nigga, just checking in on you."

"Am I dead? Did I die?" He inquired with narrowed eyes and a crunched forehead.

"Nah, you're alive." Killa Dre grinned and placed a hand on his comrade's shoulder.

"Blood, I'm high as a bitch." Banga's face winced.

"I see." Killa Dre chuckled.

"Where's Playboy at?" his head was on a swivel looking around for his sibling.

Killa Dre looked to the linoleum and took a deep breath, massaging the bridge of his nose. He tried to think of a way to break the bad news to his homeboy. When he brought his head back up and Banga saw the look in his eyes, the twin had already figured out that his brother didn't make it. Instantly, his eyes became glassy and misted with tears as his bottom lip quivered. Banga and Playboy had done everything together. They were brothers as well as best-friends. Playboy was the yin to his yang, the pen to his paper, the bullet in his gun, and the bow to his arrow. When Banga realized his brother was dead he thought he heard his heart break in two. At first he was stricken with grief, but then malice quickly poisoned his heart and he balled his hand into a fist.

"I'ma ride on them niggaz, are you with me?" Banga looked to his man, tears jetting down his cheeks as he clenched his jaws tightly. He was staring his homeboy in the eyes intensely.

"You know I'm with that one-eighty seven." Killa Dre matched the twin's intensity and extended his hand. They did a complex handshake and pounded the Blood gang sign against their chest.

"Let me get dressed, Blood, and we can...Grrrrrr." Banga grimaced as he tried to get out of the bed. The pain from his gunshot wounds surged up his torso and wreaked havoc on his body. He was halfway out of bed, and still trying to get up when Killa Dre helped him back into bed.

"Heal up first, my nigga." Killa Dre urged him, with a hand on his shoulder. "You gotta be in tiptop if we're gonna get at these buster ass niggaz, can't be no slouch. A slip up could mark your end. You feel me?"

"Yeah, I gotchu," Banga assured, grimacing as he lay back in bed trying to get comfortable, "you just be ready for when I get out, 'cause I'ma turn this city on its head looking for the mothafuckaz that blasted me and my brotha." He glared at him, nostrils flaring and jaws squared.

"I'll be ready, Blood. You just get yourself some rest." Killa Dre covered Banga up with the thin blanket. Next, he turned out the light and left out of the room, shutting the door behind him. Heading down the corridor, he could hear the sobs of his friend as he grieved over his deceased brother.

"Damn." Killa Dre cursed under his breath and shook his head, thinking how it was a shame that he'd lost another homie to the war. Throwing on his hood, he tucked his hands inside of his pockets and journeyed down the corridor.

Chapter Four

"You'll love these guys, they're cool. Trust me." Detective Dupri said to Detective De La Rosa as they stood outside the door of a white house surrounded by a picket fence. Detective Dupri was a six-one African American brother with a baldhead and a goatee. He was a born leader and considered The Alpha Male among his peers.

"I hope so, we'll see." De La Rosa said.

Detective Dupri knocked on the front door. A moment later the door was pulled open by Detective Maza. He had a Budweiser in his hand and was laughing at something one of the guys had told him before he'd opened the door.

"Well, what do we have here? Detective Marlo Dupri," Maza said, then looked to De La Rosa. "And you, I know you. I've seen you around the office before…De La Hoya, right?"

"De La Rosa." De La Rosa corrected him.

"Aye, man, get the fuck out of the way," Dupri shoved Maza aside and crossed the threshold. "Treating us like Jehovah Witnesses and shit. It's colder than Eskimo pussy outside."

"Aye, who's the new guy?" Detective Thorn asked from where he was seated at the table.

"Everyone, this is Detective Ricardo De La Rosa, homicide. He transferred to our department about three months ago. He's good people. Let me introduce you to the gang." He pointed to each man and called out there names. "This is Thorn. The dick that opened the door is Maza. This is Arsenegger. That there is Ortiz, and this is…" Dupri stopped on a gentleman sitting at the table that he'd never laid eyes on before. He was an older white man with thinning white hair, and he wore glasses. From his style of dress and the briefcase by his foot, De La Rosa figured he had to be a lawyer of some sort.

"This is my godfather." Thorn told Dupri and De La Rosa.

"Pleasure to meet you, Cheston Murphy." the lawyer introduced himself and shook both of their hands.

"Marlo Dupri." Dupri shook his hand after De La Rosa.

De La Rosa smiled on the inside when he saw that Arsenegger and Ortiz were present at the Poker game. Although he was glad that the two shady detectives were in the house, he frowned upon seeing the lawyer being there though. An innocent man wasn't part of the deal and he sure as hell didn't want to take his life. He didn't need that shit on his conscience. Something like that haunted you for the rest of your life; you'd find yourself waking up in cold sweats at night behind shit like that. He had no problem with sending everyone else to eternal damnation because they deserved it. But someone who had nothing to do with the situation was off limits to him.

De La Rosa quickly found himself with a dilemma. He thought his best bet was to wait to see if Cheston would leave earlier than Arsenegger and Ortiz so he could set off the bomb. Otherwise, he'd have to fall back and wait for another time to carrying out the hit.

"I hope you guys don't mind me sitting in on one of your games." De La Rosa said to the collective.

"You brought mula?" Detective Ortiz smiled.

"Plenty of it," De La Rosa answered jovially.

"Then mi casa su casa." Ortiz winked and took a swig of his beer.

"Have a seat, man." Dupri motioned to the chair beside De La Rosa.

De La Rosa sat his briefcase down, removed his suit's jacket and sat down in the chair.

"What's up with the briefcase?" Arsenegger nodded to the black leather briefcase De La Rosa had sat down by his foot.

"Huh?" De La Rosa looked to the briefcase. "Oh, I told my wife that I was going somewhere quiet to do our taxes when I was actually coming over here. She hates that I gamble. I don't know where my mind went; when I was getting out of the car I just grabbed this thing."

Once everyone was sitting at the table, Thorn dealt the cards and the Poker game began. The men were about fourteen hands in and De La Rosa was making sure he lost majority of them, but not noticeably. He didn't want to draw the suspicions of the men, and most importantly, he didn't want his main targets running out of cash and calling it a night.

The lawyer's cell phone rang and he took it from his hip. He pressed answer and placed the cell to his ear. "Hello? I'm over here at Toby's playing Poker with a few of the guys. Goddamn it! I'm on my way!" he put his cellular back on his hip.

"Cheston, where the hell are you going? We're in the middle of a game." Maza frowned as he complained.

"I've gotta go, I'll leave my cash in." Cheston slipped on his suits jacket.

"Is everything all right?" Dupri asked concerned.

"It's my daughter; she got arrested for a DUI." Cheston's face balled up. "Fucking kid, with all of the dough I shell out for college you'd think she'd stay out of trouble."

Thorn stood up and hugged his godfather. They broke their embrace and he told him, "Make sure you call me once you get in tonight. Love you."

"I love you, too. I'll be sure to call you." Cheston headed out of the door.

"I think I better get going, too." De La Rosa said rising from the table.

"You, too?" Maza frowned.

"My money's down, you guys can play for it." De La Rosa told them. "It's late and I got to be getting home before my old lady kills me." He shook hands with everyone sitting at the table. "It was a pleasure meeting you all." He waved on his way out of the door, closing the door behind him.

Cheston was just pulling off when De La Rosa was coming out of the house. He hopped behind the wheel of his Buick Regal and made a U-turn, heading into the opposite direction of Cheston's Benz. Once he was a block away, he took the detonator from out of the armrest and pressed the button on it.

Kaboom!

De La Rosa watched in his rearview as a huge fireball shot into the air. His eyes bugged, his heart dropped, and his stomach twisted into knots once he realized that it wasn't the house that he'd just blown up, but the vehicle Cheston had drove off in. Upon further inspection in the rearview mirror, he saw the detectives running out into the street toward the explosion.

It dawned on De La Rosa that Cheston must have picked up his briefcase thinking it was his own when he was leaving the house. De La Rosa looked away from the rearview mirror, shaking his head. He had just bought his way into hell.

$$$

"No, no," Thorn screamed at the raging fire that burned the wreckage that was Cheston's car. He could make out his burning carcass behind the wheel of the vehicle. Tears rolled down his face as he fought against Maza and Dupri who was holding him back from the fire. Giving up, Thorn hung his head and continued to weep with tears dropping from his eyes and splashing on the streets. "Oh God, Oh my God no…" he sobbed and his entire body shuddered.

Car alarms blared and neighborhood dogs barked. A fire truck and an ambulance siren wailed in the distance as they were on their way.

$$$

"How in the fuck did you miss?" Gangsta asked angrily from where he stood in Black Jesus' study.

"It was a lawyer there that had the same briefcase as me. He had to have picked mine up thinking it was his when he left." De La Rosa shook his head and ran his hand down his face. "What the fuck are the chances?" he put one hand on his hip and brushed his hair back with the other. It was apparent that he was stressed out now. Not only would the dirty detectives be on his ass, but the death of an innocent man would be on his shoulders now.

"Shit, that may have been our only chance to kill two birds with one stone." Gangsta vented and took a deep breath.

"Not necessarily." Gouch said, looking the stuffed hyena on the display dead in its eyes. "I could find out where he lay his head, walk upon him, and squeeze one through his temple. I'll make it quick and clean. Screw a silencer on the end of the barrel, and the only sound there'll be is the one his body makes when hits the ground." He continued to eyeball the hyena and maneuver the stand it was on, moving his head from left to right. Killing was a skill that Gouch honed over the years. He had become more proficient over time and grew to love it. Once he got on your trail you were as good as dead.

"Nah, I don't want there to be any links back to us when these two get dropped." Gangsta stated seriously.

Gouch stepped away from the hyena and approached his uncle. "You know my stelo, unc. No one will ever know I was there, I'll be gone with the wind."

Gangsta shook his head and gripped his nephew's shoulder. "We just got chu back, I'm not tryna chance losing you again."

"Then what do you suggest?" Black Jesus steepled his hands in his lap.

Gangsta brought his hands down his face and blew hard. "I don't know. I need some time to think."

"OK." Black Jesus nodded.

"Listen, I gotta get going, I got to get back to the office." De La Rosa said to Black Jesus as he slipped on his coat, one arm at a time. "I'm sorry about all of this, Gangsta." He patted him on the back and left out of the study.

"Fat fuck," Gangsta cursed heatedly once he was gone.

The next day

Detective Arsenegger and Ortiz were out at sea on his boat drinking cold-ones and watching the waves of the ocean. Arsenegger was dressed in a white V-neck, white linen shorts, and Louis Vuitton boat shoes while Ortiz rocked black sunglasses, a blue Lacoste sweater vest, which he wore over his bare chest to show off his toned arms, and low-top Lacoste sneakers.

"Why do you think De La Rosa would try to set us up?"

"Money, what other excuse would he need? You don't know him, and I know I sure as hell don't. So this isn't about something that we've done to him." Arsenegger was sure of this. "Someone put him up to it, and I'm betting all of my money that it's Gangsta."

"Gangsta? You think he'd have the cojones?"

"Gangsta has balls just as big as anybody that's worth mentioning in the streets. You think 'cause we wear these shields that he wouldn't take a shot at us? Especially after I promised to whack his entire family? Nah, it was definitely him, but De La Rosa is Black Jesus' bitch. He's his inside man, it makes perfect sense."

Earlier that day Arsenegger had gotten a call from Thorn saying that he'd cracked open the black leather briefcase that was left behind. Inside he'd found court documents and other paperwork, but more importantly, a name engraved at the corner inside the lid of the briefcase: Cheston Murphy. This was proof that Cheston had left with the briefcase that belonged to De La Rosa and was most likely carrying the bomb.

"What's on our agenda now?" Ortiz inquired.

"Nothing changes, we're hitting them all: Gangsta, Black Jesus, and all of their people. That's the only way I can get some fucking sleep now."

"Who's up?"

"We hit Booby tonight; find out who's on his door." Arsenegger told him. "A stack if he let's us walk through. While we're tucking him in, Thorn will be taking care of De La Rosa."

"Hello, Dupri?" Ortiz said into his cell phone. It was time to set all of the pieces of the puzzle into place.

Chapter Five

Detective Arsenegger stood at the kitchen table taking sips of a White Russian and looking over a pyramid of photographs laid out before him. Many of the black & white photographs wore red Xs on them. The photographs that wore the Xs were of the men who'd been murdered. Some of the photographs that wore the Xs were of Tango, Julio, Debo, Ridah Man, Neck Bone, Nightmare, Taco, etc. The only photograph that wore a question mark was the one of Gouch, since he'd gone missing and no one knew where to find him.

It was just as Arsenegger had thought, if he played the background for a while the players would begin to eliminate one another, and in no time he was proven right. Though many of the men had met their demise, Arsenegger reasoned he still had his work cut out for him. Not only did he have Black Jesus and his empire to bring down, but he had to keep to a promise he'd made. He'd promised Gangsta that he was going to murder his entire family, including his crew, and he aimed to keep his word.

Arsenegger stood in the full body mirror combing his hair back. He was dressed in a gray blazer and two tone Oxford shoes. Once he was done he sat the comb on the dresser and put on his Porkpie hat. He threw on his overcoat and picked up the bouquet of flowers lying on his bed. Journeying down the hallway, he met his wife as she came through the door with two brown paper bags of groceries. She was a tall slender woman with long brunette hair and ocean blue eyes. A slight sprinkle of freckles accented her nose and cheeks.

"Hey, honey." She kissed him.

"Hey, sweetheart," He responded with a toothy smile.

"Why are you all dressed up like you're going to a funeral?" She observed his attire.

"Could be that I am," he strolled out of the door.

$$$

A station wagon sat idling just outside UCLA Hospital with its headlights out. Its occupants were two unsavory characters who were as much acquainted with illicit activities as the criminals they arrested. As law enforcers their job was to rid the streets of bad guys, but on the road to accomplish this they became the very same criminals they despised. Now they were nothing more than a couple of gangsters with badges.

"Who's watching the door up there?" Arsenegger asked from the shadows of the backseat.

"Bendis."

"The rookie?"

Ortiz nodded. "He's Dupri's wife's nephew, we've already greased his palm. All you gotta do is slip in and slip out…like a cat burglar." He handed him a silenced pistol.

"What is this for?" Arsenegger asked.

"It's just in case, you never know."

Arsenegger stashed the pistol inside of his suit's jacket and hopped out of the car. When he entered the hospital the nurses' station was so crowded with visitors that they didn't notice him ease by and slip into an elevator. The elevator doors parted and he stepped out moving down the hallway. From a far he scoped a uniformed officer sitting outside a room with his face buried in The Los Angeles Times news paper. As he strolled up the officer's eyes peered over the news paper and he gave him a slight nod. Arsenegger smiled sinisterly and tipped his hat to him before pushing his way inside of the room.

$$$

All that could be heard in Pavielle's hospital room was the Beeps of the heart monitor. The room was dark save for the light illuminating his face from above his head. He lay in his cast iron-bed in a coma, hooked to tubes and an assortment of devices to monitor his vitals.

Death loomed in the atmosphere, the silhouette of the Grim Reaper moving past the wall made this evident.

A man with slicked back hair had entered Pavielle's room with a bouquet of flowers. He laid the flowers on the nightstand beside the bed and sat his hat on Pavielle's chest. "I made your uncle a promise, and I intend to keep it." Detective Arsenegger whispered into Pavielle's ear before pulling one of the pillows from behind his head and pressing it over his face, pressing down upon it.

Arsenegger spotted a red dot traveling up the side of the bed. The red dot journeyed up his torso and settled on his left-breast where his heart resided. A look of confusion ceased Arsenegger's face and he looked up to find a silhouette sitting in a chair. The light over the neighboring bed came on exposing a man perched in the chair. It was Gangsta. He wore a scowl and held a Sig Sauer in his right palm, which was equipped with an infra-red laser.

"If you don't take that pillow from my nephew's face, I'm gonna plug you with so many holes…that doctors won't know where to begin to stop the bleeding." Gangsta spoke through gritted teeth. His eyes were glassy and intimidating. His finger rested over the trigger of his weapon, ready to give a squeeze if the crooked detective disobeyed his order.

Arsenegger froze in place with an "Oh, shit" expression on his face holding the pillow over Pavielle's face. His eyes widen with fear and his mouth formed an O. All of the color drained from his face seeing the notorious drug dealer there with a banger on his ass.

"He's not gonna tell you twice," a voice came from behind Arsenegger. He would have attempted to glance over his shoulder if it wasn't for the Beretta pressed to the back of his skull. He removed the pillow from Pavielle's face and raised his hands in surrender. Gouch slowly turned him around. A thorough pat down produced a pistol with a silencer screwed on its barrel.

"What're you going to do, kill me?" Arsenegger asked with a devilish smile. "I'ma officer of the law, I'm practically untouchable."

"That's right, asshole…practically." Gouch stashed his Beretta in his waistline and struck Arsenegger across the jaw with his own gun, spilling him to the floor. He went to work kicking and stomping his mothafucking ass. Arsenegger's eyes rolled around in his head, he was dazed. Gouch pressed his sneaker to the nigga'z chest, shoved his silenced burner into his grill, and looked away as he applied pressure to the trigger. He'd just about pulled it back when Gangsta ordered him to stop.

"Fuck this grease ball mothafucka, unc." Gouch spat. He was ready to stain the waxed floor with Arsenegger's brain.

"Nah, not here, Gucci," Gangsta placed his hand on his nephew's shoulder. He then pulled Arsenegger to his feet and pressed his Sig under his chin, telling him, "If I ever catch you near my blood again, I'm going to slaughter your entire family. Do I make myself clear?" Gangsta's eyes held a glint of evil. He wanted to shoot Arsenegger so bad that his dick was hard. The crooked detective nodded his understanding. "Good. Now get the fuck outta here." He shoved him toward the door.

When Arsenegger walked out of the room, the uniformed cop that had been watching the door came inside with his gun at the ready. This was Killa Dre disguised as Dupri's wife's nephew.

"Is everything OK?" Killa Dre inquired, brows furrowed. Gangsta and Gouch nodded. "Where's old boy?"

"Restroom," Gangsta answered.

Killa Dre opened the restroom door and turned on the light. Sitting on the commode was rookie Officer Bendis in a wife-beater and boxers. He wore a sack over his head and his ankles and wrists were bound by duct-tape. His legs trembled nervously and there was a puddle of yellow fluid at his feet.

"Blood, this nigga done pissed on himself." Killa Dre shook his head, looking at the faggot ass cop pitifully. "Binem be straight pussy without a gun and a badge."

"We shouldn't have let that mothafucka go, man." Gouch brushed the top of his head with his palm. This is something he did every time he was agitated. "You and Booby tender hearted asses. He didn't want me to slump Bully and look what happened, we lost Big Head and Woo. You think Arsenegger's slimy ass gone let this ride? He's gonna come after us."

"I know that; he'll be dealt with." Gangsta said after pulling his head back in from taking a quick scan of the hallway. "I just don't wanna spill him in here. We're in a hospital full of people, there's no way we're gonna get a body outta here without them noticing. I tell you all the time to think before you react. It's a time and place for that gung-ho shit, Billy the Kid."

"What're we gonna do about Booby, man? I don't wanna leave him up here like this, that cock sucka might come back."

"I'll get Goldberg to see about moving him to another hospital, and I'll hire some security to watch his room. Just can't have Binem standing guard over him. There's no telling how deep Arsenegger's ties run with the department, especially Newton Division."

"What about this faggot?" Killa Dre asked about Bendis. He had his silver revolver pressed to his temple and was ready to nod him if his big homie gave the word.

Gangsta pulled a worn brown leather wallet from Killa Dre's back pocket. He removed Bendis's I.D and a picture of his family from it and let it fall to the floor. He pulled the sack from Bendis's head. The African American officer's eyes were bloodshot and glassy from crying. Gangsta ripped the duct-tape from his mouth, taking some of his facial hair along with it and leaving a red strip across his mouth. Bendis winced from the pain. There's was green snot bubbles forming out of his left nostril.

"Oh, God, I promise…I promise I won't say a word. Just let me…" A vicious slap across the face silenced Bendis and busted his lip.

"Shut the fuck up, and listen to what I'm about to tell you," Gangsta barked. He recited Bendis's full name and home address from his California I.D card. He then looked the picture of his family over and showed it to him. "This is a nice family you have here, Eugene. I take it that you love them."

"Yes…yes, I do." Bendis nodded as tears rolled down his face.

"I'll advise you to keep that in mind before you open your mouth about me and my friends, 'cause should any of our names come up for any reason at all, guess who's coming to dinner? Me and my pals," He threw his arm around Killa Dre's shoulder and the young boy smiled wickedly. "We're going to dismantle your children piece by piece, and then I'm gonna let junior here fuck your wife until she cums outta of her asshole, and that'll be right before he slits her throat. You copy that, Gene?"

"Yes." Bendis's voice cracked with emotions and he hung his head.

Gangsta grabbed a fistful of Bendis's hair and pulled his head up so he'd be looking directly into his eyes. "I can't hear you." He told him then turned his ear toward his mouth.

"Yes, I understand."

"Good, boy," Gangsta patted his cheek gently. "Now, once we make our exit you're gonna go back to your post like none of this ever happened, comprende?" Bendis nodded.

Snikt!

The switch-blade sounded when Killa Dre extended its blade. Bendis's eyes bugged and he looked as if he was gonna shit his trousers. "Relax. I'm only gonna cut chu loose, dawg." Killa Dre assured him.

"Unc," Gouch yelled from Pavielle's bedside.

Gangsta and Killa Dre approached Pavielle's bed, he was squeezing Gouch's hand and his eyes were fluttering.

"Gu…Gucci," he uttered through dry chapped lips.

The Lord works in mysterious way.

$$$

Ortiz was busy playing Tetris on his cell phone when he looked up and saw Arsenegger staggering down the block like an old drunk. Ortiz whipped his gun out from its holster and hopped out of the car. He rushed to Arsenegger's aide, throwing his arm over his shoulder and helping him to the car.

"What the fuck happened?" he asked concerned, sitting him in the backseat and checking him for any wounds.

"Gangsta and his nephew were up there," Arsenegger winced, making ugly faces of pain. He touched his lip and his fingers came away with blood. "They ambushed me before I could get the job done."

"Shit." Ortiz punched the backdoor in a fit and then kicked it hard as fuck. "I'm gonna see if I can catch them." He made to leave but Arsenegger grabbed him by the arm of his jacket.

"No, let'em go," Arsenegger gave him a stern look. "Let's just get outta here."

Ortiz closed the backdoor and ran around to get in on the other side.

Fourteen floors up in County General hospital, Gangsta stared down at the streets through the curtains watching as the detectives pulled away.

This shit ain't over, far from it, Gangsta thought.

The next day

"Honey, I'm home!" De La Rosa said jovially as he entered through the front door of his suburban home. He hung his coat up on the coat-hanger by the door and tossed his keys upon the coffee-table as he journeyed down the hallway calling out his wife and kids names. He checked their bedrooms and the bathroom before heading out into the backyard. Approaching the double glass sliding doors, he saw his wife and their two kids tied to chairs with black pillow cases over their heads at the swimming pool. They squirmed around in their seats, trying desperately to free themselves from their restraints. Two masked men dressed in black fatigues stood behind them: one of them had a pistol pointed to the back of the wife's head, while the other had one pointed to the back of the son and daughter's heads.

De La Rosa had a shocked expression on his face when he saw them; he pushed the sliding glass door open and drew his firearm from his shoulder holster, pointing it at the masked man standing behind his wife. "What the fuck is going on here?" he asked, ready to give the trigger a squeeze. De La Rosa was one hell of a shot, and he was sure he could hit the mothafucka standing behind his wife right between the eyes.

"Retribution," The masked man replied, "a life for a life."

Hearing that made De La Rosa's heart quicken, he instantly knew what the masked man was talking about. He even had a hunch who the men were wearing the ski-masks.

"From that look on your face, I take it you've realized who we our?" the masked man pointing his burner at the back of his wife's dome asked.

"Listen, I didn't mean for Cheston to get killed, the bomb wasn't meant for him." De La Rosa confessed looking scared as shit for his wife's life. He had a look on his face like he saw Jesus Christ appear before him or some shit.

"We know." The masked man responded. "That bomb was meant for Arsenegger and Ortiz; we were a bonus, either way you intended to kill us all."

"Please, keep my family out of this; this doesn't have anything to do with them." De La Rosa pleaded.

"Either you go, or they all go. It's as simple as that." The masked man stated firmly.

"Fine," De La Rosa pressed his pistol into his temple, indenting the skin there. His hand trembled as he held the weapon to his head. Sweat began to bead upon his forehead and roll toward his brows. He closed his eyes tightly and bit down on his bottom lip, trying to find the courage to pull the trigger. The hefty man clenched his jaws and bit down on his bottom lip hard.

"Do it!" The masked man screamed and spit flew from off of his lips.

Blam!

De La Rosa's brain exploded out the side of his skull and splattered upon the ledge of the pool, dripping off into the water below. His family thrashed around in their chairs wildly and screamed as best they could through their gags when the shot rung that ended his life. De La Rosa went face first into the swimming pool and burgundy covered the suface of the water, followed by bubbles. A third masked man stood behind him in the doorway of the glass sliding door holding a pistol. His job was to shoot De La Rosa in the back of the head if he didn't agree to off himself.

The masked man standing behind De La Rosa's wife tapped the masked man standing behind the kids and told him, "Let's go," while moving to leave.

Revenge was a dish best served cold.

Chapter Six

"They're charging you with unlawful possess of an illegal firearm and attempted murder." Goldberg informed him and adjusted his specs. He was a Jewish man of average height and a receding hairline. He wore a dark blue suit and striped tie. His nickname was "The Junkyard Dog" because he protected his clients from charges like hound would thieves from its master's business. He was a beast in the courtroom and had more connections than the back of a cable box.

"Ain't that about a bitch, the nigga tried to fit me for a suit and coffin!" Pavielle said angrily with a hoarse voice and through chapped lips. His left-wrist was handcuffed to the guardrail of the bed. A sheriff had come in earlier and read him his Miranda Rights and told him what he was under arrest for. Gangsta made a call to Artie Goldberg and he came right down. The old Jew was the family lawyer. He was at their every beck and call, this is because whenever they were in need there was money to be made.

"They have video surveillance footage of you entering his hotel room." Goldberg told him.

"Nah, nah, nah," Pavielle shook his head no. "They saw *somebody* enter his room, who's to say it was me?"

"Mr. Hood, they found you inside of Mr. Grant's hotel room with a .9mm automatic. The ballistics done on the weapon proves that the bullets found in his body were from your gun."

"What about the mothafucking slugs found in my ass, huh?" Pavielle frowned and twisted his lips.

"Unfortunately, Mr. Grant isn't alive to be brought upon charges, but you are." Goldberg pointed out.

"Whatever, fam, how much is it going to cost me to make this go away?" he asked, ready to handover whatever amount of money it would take to sweep the matter under the rug.

"Three-hundred and fifty thousand dollars and I'll see what I can do."

Before Pavielle's eyes he saw Goldberg transform into Dracula and bare his fangs. The money hungry mothafucka was a vampire, a bloodsucker. He was good at his job, but like every lawyer he tried to suck every dollar he could out of his clients. But what the fuck was Pavielle going to do? He was between a rock and a hard place, so he had to do what he had to do to guarantee that his future wouldn't be spent behind bars.

"No, for Three-hundred and fifty bands, you're gonna make this shit disappear, right?" Pavielle raised his eyebrow and gave him a stern look. Goldberg nodded in understanding if he was to take the money. He knew that if he didn't do what he said he was going to do then he could find himself in a bad way and he wasn't about to chance that. No fucking way. "I'll have my fiancé drop them ends off at your office tomorrow morning, around noon."

Goldberg left the room, and Vayda stepped into the doorway wearing a smile. Pavielle looked up at her and gave a smirk. She sat her purse on the dresser and hugged her boo, kissing him passionately. She hugged him again tightly, like if she left him go then he'd rise into the air and be carried off by the wind like a balloon. Her eyes welled up and tears spilled down her golden red cheeks.

"I've missed you so much." She told him, wiping her eyes with a curled finger.

"I've missed you, too." Pavielle confessed, the back of his hand caressing her cheek. "While I was asleep all I could do was dream about you and the baby." He rubbed on her round belly and smiled proudly. She had always beautiful to him, but he found her that more attractive being pregnant with his seed. "What do you want to name him?" He pulled a few Kleenexs from the boss beside the bed and began dabbing her face dry of the wetness.

"I don't know yet, I was hoping that you had a name in mind." She sniffled as he dried her checks.

Pavielle chuckled and said, "That's a damn shame, we don't know what we're going to name our son." He balled up the Kleenexs that he used to dab her cheeks with and rested his hand on his lap.

"We still got time." Vayda smiled. "We'll come up with a name before he's here." She looked up at his frizzy cornrows and played with his hair. "Your shits looking bad, boo. I gotta comb and a jar of Vaseline in my bag; I'ma hook you up, okay?"

"Bool."

She retrieved a comb and a small jar of Vaseline from her purse. She stuffed an extra pillow behind her fiancé, which she'd gotten from off the other bed, to prop his head up. Grimacing, Pavielle slid over to the right as much as his handcuffed hand and wounds would allow. Vayda parted his hair and slicked Vaseline down the visible skin, beginning the task of braiding his hair. Pavielle watched the police officer that was there to guard his door.

This mothafucka is like a guard dog, Pavielle thought. *Strip him of his gun and his badge and what do you have? A pussy! A lily white pussy, there's no way he could survive in these streets. Look at him.* He shook his head at the scrawny and nerdy uniformed officer that was wearing a hard face. He was trying to mirror toughness, but the young kingpin read him like a good book. It was the experiences in life that hardened a man and prepared him for harsh times, experiences that the officer was trying to display with a mean mug that had to be shown with heart and balls. Your eyes reflected your road through life not the expression your face projected.

"So, what is the lawyer talking about?" Vayda asked.

"Money," Pavielle answered. "That's what all of those cock suckas talk about. That's all they understand?"

"I'ma need you to drop off three-hundred and fifty bands to his office." Pavielle told her. "He said they're gonna book me into The Towers, but I want chu to be ready with that bail money 'cause I'm not tryna sit there any longer than I have to."

"You know your lady got chu. Ride or die." She held out the inside of her wrist, showing off the tattoo in fancy lettering: Ride of die. Pavielle boasted the same tattoo which he'd also gotten on the inside of his wrist. They'd gotten the ink the day after they were engaged. It was a way of showing their loyalty to one another.

"Ride or die." He repeated as she leaned closer and kissed him.

"That's messed up that you still gotta go to jail, though"

"Yeah, that's just the process. But Goldberg's gonna make this whole thing go up in smoke. Fucking Jew costs an arm and a leg, but with his connections it's well worth it."

Pavielle grew still and quiet for a moment. Vayda glanced at him and could tell that he was thinking about something. "What's on your mind, baby?"

"All of the things I gotta deal with once I touch these streets." He admitted. "It's one headache after the other when you're in the thick of this shit."

Once Pavielle had come out of his coma and shook the fog that clouded his brain, he was brought up to speed on everything that had occurred since he was held captive within the confines of his mind. He was told about the recent reemergence of a foe that was proving to be more of a nuisance than Nightmare ever was. He was ten times as worse and willing to go the extra mile and then some. Pavielle knew that Paybacc was going to be more than a handful, which meant he had his work cut out for him. He knew that these kinds of situations came with being a boss and he had to rectify them as quickly as possible.

Then there was crooked ass Detective Arsenegger. He snuck into his room like a thief in the night and tried to steal his life. Not to mention, he tried to have his entire crew and set eradicated. When the idea of murking Arsenegger was first brought to the attention of Pavielle, he brushed it off. He couldn't entertain the idea of murdering a cop, but this time it was different. That crooked ass Arsenegger was trying to kill him, so he had no choice but to kill him. It wasn't any way around it. He had to treat homeboy like he'd treat an enemy of his hood. From now on it was T.O.S: Terminate on Sight. So if he saw him in traffic in that Crown Vic, then he was lighting that mothafucka up. Straight like that. There was no doubt in his mind. He didn't give a mad ass fuck. He had a family to take care of and he was going to make sure he was alive to do it.

"Heavy is the head that wears the crown." Vayda said, braiding her man's hair.

"You can say that again." Pavielle stared ahead at nothing.

$$$

"For three-hundred and fifty kay he better make this shit poof into smoke." Gouch looked over his shoulder at Goldberg as he headed out of the waiting room. Gangsta had just sat down after talking to him and told him how much he was charging Pavielle to handle his charges. Although Goldberg was a good lawyer, like his little brother, Gouch despised his money grubbing ass. He felt that he was all about his money, which was OK, but he thought he should show some humanity behind it. "Fucking paper gangsta," He shook his head shamefully.

"It's cool. Just as long as dude gets Booby off, I'm not tripping." Gangsta patted him on the back. "Even if it costs a million to guarantee my nephew's freedom, I'd pay it. I'd cash-out every time."

"Look at this nigga," Gouch smiled at pointed at a sleeping Killa Dre. He was laid back in his chair with his head cocked to the side, drooling out of the corner of his mouth. His saliva dripped on to his shirt and created a dark wet spot.

Gangsta smiled and shook his head. "Lil' homie is tired. Long days and even longer nights: the life of a hustla. I know it all too well."

Gouch picked a few nuts from his bag of Planters cashew nuts and started throwing them at Killa Dre, trying to land one inside of his mouth. One landed inside of the young nigga'z grill and he gagged. He quickly sat up and rubbed his throat, looking around shocked with his bloodshot and glassy eyes. He spotted Gouch and Gangsta laughing and knew that they did something to him.

"Why are you niggaz playing, Blood?" he scowled, picking up the cashews that littered his shirt and threw them at Gouch and Gangsta. It didn't faze them because they kept right along laughing. Pissed off, Killa Dre pulled his jacket over his head and went back to sleep.

"I'ma run down stairs real quick and grab me something out of one of these vending machines." Gangsta informed his oldest nephew as he rose to his feet.

"I'm coming with you, I want something to drink." Gouch followed behind him.

Gangsta and Gouch looked over the outside vending machines trying to see what they wanted to purchase. Gangsta winded up getting a Minute Maid apple juice and a turkey sandwich, while Gouch settled on an A&W Root Beer. They turned to leave but froze in their tracks once they found a threesome of men before them. They all wore hard faces except for the muscular one. He was the first to speak.

"Well, isn't it big bad Gangsta from Eastside Rolling 20s." Paybacc smiled, boasting his infamous gold capped tooth. "What's cracking, Outlaw? Long time no see, homie." Gangsta and Gouch's faces twitched with anger. He addressed Gouch. "You must be Gouch, I've heard so much about chu. Word is you're about putting in that work. I must tip my hat to you, my nigga; from one killa to anotha. Salute," He saluted Gouch. Paybacc noticed Gouch and Gangsta's hands moving toward their waistlines where their bangers were stashed. The smile vanished from his face and was replaced with one of seriousness. "If y'all niggaz wanna get stupid then we can get downright fucking retarded." He said from the confines of his wheelchair, his thick, muscular neck moving between the uncle and nephew. He'd been sitting in it when he was rolled through the metal-detector to thwart attention from the guns he had stashed within the recesses of his hefty jacket. His hands were resting on the armrests, but Domino and Wacko were ready to draw on Gouch and Gangsta. "I'd much rather not dumb out in this bitch, especially with the boys present." He nodded to the right where a couple of cops were drinking coffee and indulging in Danishes inside of the hospital cafeteria.

Gangsta spared a glance at the cops and tapped Gouch, letting him know that the law was definitely in the house. Gouch let his hand fall to his side. Domino and Wacko lowered their hands as well. "If you're not here to spill blood, then what the fuck do you want then?"

"I'm here to offer you a proposition." Paybacc lie back in his wheelchair and put his finger tips and thumbs together.

"Go on." Gangsta told him.

"Gimmie Booby and this whole thing is over. It's just as simple as that."

"You're outta your fucking mind if you think we're…" Gouch was cut short by Gangsta nudging him.

"Not a fucking chance. This thing is bigger than you and I, homeboy. I lost my moms, my friends, and countless homies behind this here. So this thing ain't over until a smoking gun is in my hand and your dead body is at my feet. Booby and Nightmare may have started this, but it's you and I who are going to finish it. And I put that on Blood Gang." He stared into Paybacc's eyes with murderous intentions. He wanted to say fuck it and dumb-out, but he had to be the rational thinker amongst he and Gouch. He had made his sister a promise to take care of his nephews until he lay beside her in the dirt, so he was still obligated to his responsibility, even though Pavielle and Gouch were grown.

Paybacc shrugged and threw up his hands like OK, I *tried to compromise.* "If that's how you wanna play it, cuz. Just remember it's your funeral…as well as your loved ones." Paybacc mad dogged them both before swinging his wheelchair around and rolling off. Domino and Wacko slowly stepped backwards with their hands lingering near their weapons. Once they were sure Gangsta and Gouch weren't going to make a move, they hurried off behind Paybacc.

"You see that shit, Blood?" Gouch asked Gangsta after Paybacc and his minions had parted. "This mothafucka is on top of us. We gotta find out where these niggaz lay at and wet'em up."

Gangsta nodded in agreement and said, "Come on, let's get back up stairs."

Paybacc and his dogs had to go; there's wasn't any questioning it.

Chapter Seven

Detective Arsenegger sat perched on a stool nursing a glass of his favorite drink, White Russian. In his mind his thoughts were in labor trying to birth a master plan that would enable him to get rid of all of his adversaries at once: Gangsta, Gouch, Pavielle and Black Jesus. He knew he wouldn't be able to have a peace of mind until he was relieving himself upon their tombstones. He didn't know what his strategy was going to be, but it was going to have to be epic if he was going to rid Los Angeles of some of its most belligerent gangsters.

Ever since he was a kid playing cops and robbers with his older brother, Detective

Ryan Arsenegger dreamt of being a police officer. His father was a cop, his father's father was a cop, and his old man before him wore the shield. It was a family tradition for the Arseneggers to be in law enforcement, so it didn't come as a surprise when Ryan entered the academy.

Ryan dived into the game headfirst not knowing exactly what he was getting himself involved in. His father and grandfather had told him some pretty scary stories about their experiences in the streets, but nothing could prepare him like experiences of his own. The job was more hectic than he expected, and he was under more stress than he imagined. Not to mention he'd almost been killed on more than one occasion. Over time the occupational hazard of a law enforcer began to wear on Ryan and he slowly began to change.

Four years in and he became somewhat of a Boogeyman for criminals. He reasoned that to catch the bad guy you had to become him or something worse. He believed it had to be done even if it meant losing your identity in the process, because if not the world would come to destroy its self and everyone in it.

Arsenegger downed the last of his White Russian and knocked the glass of ice on the bar-top, trying to get the bartender's attention. A burly man with a balding scalp and black rings around his eyes turned around cleaning out a beer mug with a rag. Done cleaning the beer mug, he hung it above the bar along with the others.

"Jesus, another one? This will be your fifth one in the past hour." The bartender commented on him wanting another drink. "What do ya have? A vendetta against your liver or something?"

Arsenegger pulled out a cigarette from the wrinkled pack that was in his breast pocket and slid it between his thin, pink lips. Cigarette hanging from the corner of his mouth, he said, "Aye, Ned, do me a favor, will ya?" he took the time to light his cancer stick, took a puff, and then blew smoke. "Shut your fat fucking mouth and get my drink! If I wanted shit about my drinking I'd go to Alcoholics Anonymous. Hurry along now, chop! Chop!" he clapped the bar-top.

"You want your drink? I get chu your fucking drink." The bartender mumbled under his breath as he turned his back on Arsenegger and smacked the glass down. He went about the task of making the White Russian. He poured Vodka, coffee liqueur and milk into the glass. He glanced over his shoulder to see if Arsenegger was watching him and he wasn't. So he spat in his drink and stirred it up. Turning around, he approached Arsenegger with a smile and sat his drink in front of him. "Sorry, about that earlier, this ones on the house," He told his shady ass.

A tall, slender black kid in a snapback Red Sox cap and square diamond earrings too big for his earlobes came strolling into the bar with two other guys and three chicks. Arsenegger was just about to take a sip of his drink, but stopped the glass at his lips once he saw them in the large mirror behind the bar. He was focused on the tall black kid in the snapback rocking the over sized diamond earrings. He had an eerie resemblance to Gouch, especially once he started laughing with the others when one of the guys he was with told a joke. Arsenegger imagined that the kid was Gouch, and that he was laughing at him after pummeling him back at the hospital.

Arsenegger sat his drink down and felt the stitches above his brow compliments of the lanky thug. Remembering how that nigga Gouch had whipped his ass pissed him off. Malice poisoned his heart and he clenched his teeth, causing his tightened jaw to twitch. Before he knew it the black kid was standing beside him ordering a pitcher of beer. He threw his head back saying "what's up?" to Arsenegger and tossed back a few beer nuts as he patiently waited for his pitcher.

Arsenegger turned around to him on his stool and said, "Aye, don't put your fucking hands on me! I'ma officer of the law, buddy!"

Porno looked around confused. He wasn't for sure if Arsenegger was speaking to him or not. "Yo, what the fuck are you talking about?"

Arsenegger looked around to make sure no one was watching him and then said, "OK, that's it, asshole! I'm running you…" he stopped and whipped his head back as if Porno had punched him. "Motherfucker!" he swung around and punched the young man in the jaw, dropping him to the floor. "Stop resisting arrest!" he shouted, kicking and stomping him on the kid. Seeing his victim's friends running up on him at the corner of his eye, Arsenegger drew his weapon from its holster and turned on them. "Back the fuck up! This man is under arrest for assaulting an officer of the law!"

"What the fuck?!" one of the guys said in disbelief.

"Hey, man, he never touched you; I was watching him the entire time." The other guy added.

"Well, if you were, how did you miss him throw that sucker punch?" Arsenegger handcuffed Porno and pulled him to his feet. Porno's legs were like Jello under him. He could barely stand. On top of that, he had two knots on his forehead, his right-eye was swollen shut and he was bleeding from his lip. Arsenegger had done a number on him.

Arsenegger escorted Porno outside and threw him into the backseat of his Crown Victoria. He resurrected the engine and drove off with the kid talking shit in the backseat. "Old crooked ass mothafucking cops, man! Y'all think y'all are gonna keep getting away with this type of shit?!" Porno locked eyes with Arsenegger through the rearview mirror for a moment. A light bulb of recognition came on inside of his head. "Wait a minute, I thought I knew your trifling ass. Boy tonight is not your night. See, you fucked around and violated the wrong nigga. I got something for your punk ass. When I'm done with you, you'll be down on your knees with a revolver in your mouth ready to end it all." He spat blood on the floor.

The Crown Victoria came to an abrupt halt. Arsenegger threw it in park and turned to the backseat. "Oh, you threatening me, cock sucker?" he barked, climbing over the backseat punching a defenseless Porno in the face and head until he was exhausted. Once he was done he wiped his bleeding knuckles off with some napkins from the glove-box and pulled off.

Arsenegger drove Porno to an alley that sat between two abandoned warehouses where he kicked his ass some more and left him lying unconscious. After handing down a beating to the guy, he felt slightly better about the thrashing Gouch gave him.

$$$

Domino and Wacko sat at the kitchen table chopping up tan crack rocks, weighing them, and then bagging them up. The Saran Wrap from two blocks of cocaine lay strewn on the table among cocaine residue and black digital scales.

Paybacc lay on the couch watching TV in a wife-beater stained with spaghetti and sweat pants. His Calico M950 lie on the coffee-table next to a bowl stained with pasta, a half empty bottle of Heineken, a wrinkled pack of Newport 100s and an ashtray littered with butts. He laughed his head off at the antics of Lucy that played out on the screen before him.

"Cuz, we definitely gone need some more work." Domino told Paybacc. "These are the last two bricks we got to work with and the homies have damn near burned through that other shit."

"Yeah, I know. I'ma get on the jack with Creeper in a minute." Paybacc busted up laughing all of a sudden while looking at TV. "You wasn't lying though, Loco. That spic got some exceptional work on deck."

"I told you." Domino reminded him.

"This time I'ma double up on these niggaz." He told him his plans, never taking his eyes away from the TV screen. "Once we dead Booby and his people, we can get this money without any distractions. Shit will be lovely then."

"Fa' sho'."

"Man, I gotta take a shit." Paybacc frowned after hearing his stomach grumbling. He snatched his cell phone off of the charger in the corner of the living room and made for the bathroom. Once he'd gone, Wacko tapped Domino on his arm.

"We should just say fuck it and slump him while he's on the shitter." The little nigga suggested to Domino. "He left his gat on the coffee-table, so he'll be at our mercy."

"Nah, the deal was to wait until he gets his re-up. You heard him say he was gone double up, right? That's twenty of them thangs we can flip; all profit. We can eat, and good, too."

"I'm just saying, cuz."

"I got this." Domino assured him. "His time is coming; you just play your position until then, all right?"

Wacko blew hard and nodded his head.

His patience was wearing thin.

Chapter Eight

The sun rose over the horizon bullying the night and shedding its light over the city streets. People were out and about leaving and coming to their destinations, or waiting on buses and flagging down taxis to get to them. The day was like any other day for many people except for a chosen few and Pavielle Hood. Today he was being released from Twin Towers County Jail. He had only been there for a few hours. It wasn't long enough for the foreign stench to embed in his skin and warrant a bath, but he was going to take one anyway once he'd gotten home. He was in dire need of one seeing how he'd only been given sponge baths during the past couple of months he was in the hospital. It was one of the few things he longed for and missed since he drifted into a coma. But it would have to wait because he had more pressing matters to attend to before he took care of his hygiene.

Pavielle stepped out through the doors of The Twin Towers with the support of his Oakwood cane. He took his time making his way to the corner where a group of pigeons congregated. A red H2 Hummer came to a halt at the corner disturbing the pigeons. The feathery creatures flew off in all directions flapping their wings and leaving feathers floating around in the air. The rays of the sun blinded Pavielle as he approached the backdoor of the hog. He raised a hand over his brows to block the illumination, idling behind the Hummer were three more vehicles of all make and models. Stashed inside were hardheads armed to the teeth looking to earn recognition and a check along with it. Pavielle smiled. He had goons on deck and pitied the poor bastards that would dare try to make a move on him that day. They were sure to be turned into Swiss cheese along with whatever whip they were in. He was confident that the weapons his shooters were packing could turn any vehicle into the car Bonnie and Clyde got caught slipping in.

Pavielle opened the backdoor, tossed his cane inside, and climbed in. Slamming the door closed, he gave the hog the once over. Occupying the vehicle were Gangsta, Gouch and Vayda, who was sitting in the backseat with him.

"Hey, baby." She greeted and kissed him on the cheek.

Pavielle frowned and looked up front to Gangsta and Gouch. "Fuck is she doing here? Y'all know all of the shit we got popping out here, with all of these mothafuckaz tryna kill us. You know that she's carrying my seed. Y'all putting two lives in jeopardy with her being here."

"My fault, Booby," Gouch said from behind the wheel. "She begged me to come along to pick you up. I turned simp and gave in. My bad, Blood."

Pavielle sighed and looked to Vayda.

"I'm sorry, baby. Don't be mad at Gucci, be mad at me." Vayda pleaded with him. "I really wanted to see you, boo. I mean I almost lost you…we almost lost you." She corrected herself and placed Pavielle's hand on her belly. This made him brighten up. He smiled as he rubbed his lady's protruding stomach, kissing it lovingly.

"Good morning, prince." Pavielle spoke to his unborn child. "Have you been taking care of the kingdom in my absence?" he placed his ear to Vayda's belly and his eyes lit up. "He kicked! I think he heard me." He looked to his boo smiling.

Vayda smiled as she rubbed the side of her man's face, staring deep into his brown eyes. "I love you, Pavy."

"I love you, too." He kissed her.

"Soft ass nigga," Gouch laughed.

"Shut up, Gucci!" Vayda nudged Gouch in the head. "You always got something to say."

"Don't mind me, bro." Gouch told Pavielle. "I'll leave the loving to you, and you leave the killing to me and the girls." He referred to his twin Berettas. He'd gotten himself a new pair once he got back into the thick of things.

"Yeah, whatever, nigga," Pavielle looked over the insides of the hummer. He knocked on the window, it was solid. "Shit bulletproof. Did Gizmo armor all of your whips?"

"Yep, and they all have stash spots for them thangz, too." Gangsta let it be known. He motioned for Pavielle to lean forward with his finger. Pavielle leaned forward as far as his wounds would allow. He watched as Gangsta pushed a button that ejected a secret compartment that exposed a black .9mm automatic. He passed the handgun to the backseat. Pavielle took the .9mm and tucked it into his waistline.

Gangsta pressed the button again and the compartment closed. "Sweet, huh?"

"Hell yeah, Binem will never think to look in there for a strap." Pavielle was impressed.

"We're getting all of your cars fitted with the same shit. We're on our way to Gizmo's now to pick up your whips." Gangsta informed him.

"Bool," the young kingpin lay back in the seat. Vayda laid her head into his lap and closed her eyes. He played with her hair as he stared out of the limousine tinted window at the scenery, watching it change before his eyes.

"Alright, this is it." Gouch pulled the Hummer up to the curb outside of Gizmo's Auto and Repair shop. He hopped out and Gangsta followed suit.

Pavielle hopped out and closed the backdoor on Vayda as she was trying to hop out. "Unh unh, you stay inside; you're carrying the most valuable treasure in this world. And I'll be damned if I let a nigga take that from me." Vayda giggled and smiled. He kissed her and motioned for the black Mercedes Benz that had the Muslims as its cargo. Nasheed and his men filed out of the vehicle and moved in formation to protect his queen. With quick motions of his finger, Nasheed directed the Muslims on where to stand around the Hummer to shield Vayda. The Muslims took the left, right, back and front of the Hummer.

Nasheed gave a stern look and nod to Pavielle letting him know that he had everything under control. Pavielle returned the nod and walked toward the auto shop with Gangsta and Gouch. Entering the garage of the auto shop, the threesome saw sparks flying as a crew of Mexican men was hard at work on cars wielding, adding tires, and sound systems among other things. A tall dude rocking an unkempt afro, a bushy mustache, and thick eyeglasses approached them from the left wiping his hands with an oil stained rag. He was dressed in a navy blue Dickie suit and steel-toe boots.

"I take it you're here to pick up your toys?" Gizmo said to the threesome.

"Yeah," Pavielle nodded.

"Follow me." Gizmo motioned for them to follow him. He led them into a darker area of the huge garage, which was hidden in the confines of a shadow. He pressed in a combination on the digital keypad and the shutter rose, exposing a secret garage loaded with cars of all makes and models. These were the vehicles of the men and women in the underworld who'd come in to have their vehicles bulletproofed and installed with secret compartments to hide illegal possessions. One of the most famous jobs that Gizmo was known for were dummy gas-tanks. Hustlers would come to get the dummy gas tanks installed because they could use it to hide their work in whenever they were going out of town to re-up.

Gizmo showed Pavielle his Mercedes Benz CLK and his cherry red Chevrolet Impala. He had bulletproofed them all and equipped them with stash spots. Gizmo opened the doors of both vehicles and allowed Pavielle to make a thorough inspection of them both. Pavielle made his way around to the front of his Mercedes Benz and drew his .9mm automatic from his waistline. He took aim at the windshield of the luxury vehicle while Gangsta, Gouch and Gizmo were discussing the work he'd done on the cars.

Bloc! Bloc! Bloc! Bloc!

The barrel of Pavielle's weapon erupted as it ejected hollow tip slugs, startling Gangsta, Gouch and Gizmo. The gunshots echoed throughout the garage and the empty shell casings hit the floor smoking. Pavielle lowered his .9mm automatic to his side and smirked seeing that he was only able scratch the surface of his whip with the slugs. He nodded his head in approval and looked over to Gangsta, Gouch and Gizmo. They were all wearing shocked expressions.

"This shits official." Pavielle tucked his .9mm automatic on his waistline and approached Gizmo, slapping hands and embracing him. "I see you haven't gotten sloppy, you do good work, Giz."

"Thanks." Gizmo pushed his glasses back upon his face. Gouch shoved a crinkled brown paper bag of money into his possession and he peered inside. He picked up one of the rubber-band stacks out of the brown paper bag, licked his thumb, and flickered through the bills. Satisfied, he dropped the stack back into the brown paper bag.

"We good?" Gangsta inquired.

Gizmo gave him a thumb up and shook all of their hands.

"Gucci, I'll whip the Benzo, you roll the Chevy back." Gangsta ordered.

"I wanna pick up some flowers and push out to Inglewood Cemetery. I haven't seen G-momma, my moms, and pops in a while." Pavielle told his uncle.

"Yeah, me either." Gouch draped his arm over his brother's shoulders.

"Alright, bet." Gangsta caught the car keys when Gizmo tossed them to him. "We can get two of the homies to roll these then." He pulled his cellular from off of his waistline and placed his call.

After picking up triplet bouquet of flowers, Pavielle and company rolled out to Inglewood Cemetery. A band of shooters stood out by the vehicles keeping an eye on things while the Muslims accompanied Booby and his family to his relatives' graves. After laying the flowers on G-momma, Robin, and Joshua's graves, Pavielle stood looking over their grave-stones. His eyes welled up as a collage of memories invaded his thoughts. Tears spilled over the rims of his eyes and down his cheeks. He wiped his face with his sleeve and Gouch draped his arm over his shoulder for comfort.

"Are you, all right?" Gouch asked his baby brother.

Pavielle nodded his head and said, "I'm good."

"I love you, bro."

"I love you, too."

Vayda interlocked her fingers with Pavielle's and leaned her head against his shoulder as she became teary eyed.

"Yo, Booby," A voice called out to Pavielle. Everyone looked to where the voice came and saw Gangsta. He waved them all over and they started in his direction. Approaching, Pavielle saw that his uncle was standing before Nightmare's tombstone. His sadden expression quickly converted to one of hatred. Unconsciously, he found himself biting down on his bottom lip and balling his fists. He stood face to face with the tombstone of the man that had killed countless of his homies, rape and murdered his grandmother, and nearly made his unborn child a bastard. It was safe to say that he hated

Nightmare more than he hated any of his enemies, and there weren't many of them alive to speak of.

"Bitch ass nigga, I beat chu, pussy. I won!" Pavielle harped up a glob of saliva and spat it on Nightmare's tombstone. The Muslims exchanged glances and whispered among one another, they didn't agree with what he had done. Gouch and Gangsta just stood there with frowns plastered on their faces. They both understood the hatred that Pavielle had in his heart for the infamous gangster because they had it in theirs, too.

Pavielle took his arm away from Vayda and stepped to Nightmare's tombstone. He unzipped his jeans and pulled out his meat. Feeling that he was going too far, Nasheed made to protest, but Gangsta cut him off and shook his head. With a sinister smile, Pavielle relieved himself on Nightmare's tombstone and grave. Once he was done, he gave his dick two shakes and put it back into his jeans. For a time he watched the yellow fluid run over his enemy's tombstone, feeling a sense of accomplishment. Pavielle interlocked his fingers with Vayda and turned to walk away, with everyone following suit.

That night

Vayda lay on her side in bed snuggled under the covers. The door opened cutting a ray of light through the darkness of the bedroom. Pavielle closed the door behind him and made his way over to the bed. He'd spent the past few hours with Gangsta and Gouch smoking weed and drinking cups of hard liquor while chopping it up. He pulled his .9mm automatic from his waistline and stashed it under his pillow. Next, he sat down on the bed and leaned his cane against the wall on the side of the dresser. He carefully peeled off his shirt and tossed it aside on the floor. He then slowly brought his legs over into the bed and leaned against the headboard.

Vayda turned over in bed. She kissed on Pavielle's chest around his healing gunshot wounds while her hand unbuckled and unzipped his jeans. She dipped her hand into his boxer-briefs caressing his length and causing him to draw wood, as she sucked on his neck and pulled gently on his bottom lip. She could taste the lingering Hennessy on his bottom lip.

Pavielle moaned softly feeling good, his eyes fluttered and he licked his top lip as Vayda planted hickeys on his neck. "Wha…What are you doing?" he stammered.

"What do you think I'm doing?" she asked in a sensual whisper.

"Babe, I don't think I'm quite ready for this, I'm still a lil' sore," He confessed with his eyes closed, enjoying her fondling of him.

"It's cool, I got chu." Vayda assured him. She straddled him and pulled her panties to the side, exposing her fat kitty cat which was already warm and wet. Pavielle licked his lips at the anticipation of feeling her soaking walls as he held his dick at the base. Vayda hovered over the throbbing head of hid grown man, dripping her juices over it and his hand. She slowly brought her vagina to meet his head and they absorbed one another, fitting each other like a tailor made glove. They both gasped as their sexes united as one, beginning a journey on what was to be some of the best sex either of them had experienced. Pavielle leaned his head back and gripped Vayda's waist as she grinded on him, slowly and then eventually faster. She was careful to make sure she had all of his length buried deep inside of her pussy. Once she had found a pace and rhythm that she was pleased with, she worked her hips intensely causing them both to moan in bliss.

Pavielle's hands slipped themselves under her silk gown and found her breasts. They'd gotten bigger since she became pregnant and that turned him on even more. He groped them like an old pervert and she loved it. It caused her nipples to harden and her face to twist into an ugly expression as if an evil spirit had floated across the bedroom and absorbed into her body. She grunted animalistic like. Looking down at her lover's face, she saw that he was enjoying it and she threw her head back. She closed her eyes and rode him faster. The noises of their love making sounded like two wild beasts going at it in the depths of a dark, wet jungle. Vayda dug her manicured nails into Pavielle's shoulders and stared down at him sneering. She was fucking him like she hated his guts now and it was so good. Pavielle pushed her arms aside and grabbed her by her throat, giving her a slight choke. He gripped her hip so tight that redness formed around his hand.

Staring up at her, he drove his cock inside of her as hard and as deep as he could, causing her to whine in pleasure. Heavy breathing from the two of them flooded the bedroom and before long they were drenched in one another's nectars.

When Vayda exploded the veins that had formed on her forehead and neck disappeared, and her once angry face was now smiling. She giggled and leaned closer, kissing Pavielle passionately as her sandy brown curls hung in his face. She climbed off of him and snuggled beside him, tucked snugly under his right-arm. They both closed their eyes and drifted off to sleep.

$$$

Porno sat at the small desk in his dorm room. The only light was the only one illuminating from the desk lamp so he wouldn't awaken his slumbering roommate. He packaged video-tapes and addressed them to various news stations. Porno had taken quite the beating from Arsenegger and his damages were the testament. His right-eye was swollen shut, his lip was split and tiny cuts were littered his face. He wore a neck-brace and a cast on his right-foot and left-arm. His crutches were propped against his desk as he handled the task at hand.

"Yeah, let's see how your cracka ass like these apples." Porno laughed and kissed the video-tape he'd just packaged. He slapped a postage stamp at the corner of it and turned out the desk lamplight. Come tomorrow morning he was going to drop off all of the packages at the post office to be mailed.

This was going to be one man that Arsenegger wasn't going to regret fucking with.

Chapter Nine

The next day

Killa Dre was slumped behind the wheel of his black Dodge Charger with the white leather seats. His camouflage bucket hat sat over his eyes and his arms were folded to his chest. His right-hand gripped his banger tightly, which was hiding in his armpit out of sight. At first glance it would appear that the young boy was asleep, but looks are very deceiving. If some fool thought he was gone creep up and jack him for his ride he was in for a rude awakening. He would get a wakeup call in the form of seven .357 Magnum bullets.

Meek Mill's Dreams & Nightmares CD played softly from his speakers. Killa Dre was parked outside of Harbor General hospital. He had gotten a call from Banga saying that he needed someone to pick him up from the hospital once he was released. Banga being his nigga and all, Killa Dre told him that he'd pick him up. Twenty minutes later, the young nigga was pulling into the parking lot of Harbor General hospital. He'd bought himself a double cheese burger and fries from In and Out up the street. Once he'd finished his meal he noticed that fifteen minutes had already passed, and before he knew it, he'd been waiting for two hours.

Tap! Tap! Tap!

The window glass sounded as someone knocked on it, prompting Killa Dre to point his silver revolver at the passenger side window. Seeing the weapon caused Banga to jump back with his hands in the air.

"Chill, Blood, it's me." Banga told him. Killa Dre lowered his revolver and unlocked the passenger side door. Banga opened the door and eased himself inside. He closed the door to and slapped hands with his nigga. "My bad, fam, I know you've been waiting out here for a minute. It took forever for them to release me and for me to get this medicine and shit." He held up the brown paper bag of his pain medication.

"Don't wet it." Killa Dre pulled the seatbelt across his person and locked it. He then resurrected the engine and pulled out of the parking stall. Having looked both ways, he pulled out into the street making a left and heading down Carson street.

"Blood, I can't believe you're driving with no Ls." Banga smirked. "Binem ain't pulled you over yet?"

"Nah, and even if they did I'm straight. Gangsta gotta hookup at the DMV that plugged my shit in." Killa Dre informed him.

"That's what's up." Banga nodded.

Killa Dre pulled into a Chevron gas station and executed the engine. He made to hop out, but Banga tapping his arm caused him to stop.

"Let me give you some snaps on the petro." He dipped into the pocket of his jeans and pulled out a wad of wrinkled dead white people.

"Nah, you good, B. You know how we do." Killa Dre closed the door shut and mobbed into the Chevron gas station.

Once Killa Dre had gone, Banga fished around into the ashtray, which was a graveyard for cigarette butts, until he found a roach. He put the roach into his mouth, grabbed a lighter, and put fire to the end of it. He took a couple of pulls, blew out the smoke and sucked it back in. He then blew the smoke out again and took another pull. Hearing a noise at his rear, he adjusted the side-view mirror and spotted two young chicks. One was slim with a honey complexion and blonde hair, while the other was the color of a walnut and rocked her hair shaved on one side like the singer Cassie. The chicks were handing a couple of flyers to some guys that had just pulled into the gas station. After speaking with them for a moment they made their way in Banga's direction. He smiled as he checked out their profiles through the side-view mirror. Both of the chicks were easy on the eyes, but he was really feeling old girl with the blonde mop.

"What it do, big daddy?" Blondie asked seductively, licking her pink lipstick lips and hanging inside of the passenger side window. The way she was eying Banga made his dick jump in his jeans. He wondered what those full lips of hers would feel like wrapped around his pole.

"Whatever I tell it to." Banga responded confidently. He looked her up and down.

"I heard that, why don't chu bring it down to Clug Mack Daddy tonight and watch me perform." She handed Banga a flyer for the event but he barely paid it any attention.

Blondie took the roach from Banga's lips and took a pull, blowing smoke out the corner of her mouth.

"So what's your name, sweetheart?" Banga asked. Sneaking a peek through the rearview mirror he saw Killa Dre macking Blondie's homegirl while he pumped the gas.

"Candy Cane." She smiled and giggled.

"Candy Cane, I'm Banga." He introduced himself and shook her hand.

"It's a pleasure to meet chu, Banga."

"Oh, the pleasure is all mine." He licked his lips as he admired her beauty. She was a ghetto fine dime with an ass too big for her frame. Banga could tell she must have gotten butt injections, but he didn't care because little momma had a crazy body and mad sex appeal.

"So are you gonna come see me tonight, Banga?" she asked as she toyed with the hefty charm hanging from around his neck that spelled out his name in gold and diamonds.

"Two sho', lil' momma, maybe we can slide somewhere else afterwards." He licked his lips and bit down on the bottom one, eying her hungrily.

"No doubt," Candy Cane kissed two of her fingers and pressed them against Banga's lips. She waved goodbye as she walked off leaving him with a rock hard dick. Banga leaned out of the window watching as Candy Cane and her homegirl walked off. He bit down on his bottom lip again as her juicy ass swayed from left to right and caused her miniskirt to rise and expose the bottoms of her butt cheeks. He imagined his face buried deep inside of her snatch as he ate her out from behind.

Killa Dre hopped back inside and slammed the door closed. He programmed Candy Cane's friend's number into his cell phone before returning it to his waistline and resurrecting the engine. He pulled off with Banga studying the flyer that Candy Cane had given him.

"Mothafucka," Banga said under his breath as he looked over the flyer.

"What's bracking?" Killa Dre asked as he ate a Honey Bun.

"This is the bitch! This is the bitch that capped my brother!" Banga hollered, jabbing his finger at the flyer. A half naked Passion was on the front of the flyer as the headline of Club Mack Daddy that weekend. "She was there with Paybacc and that other broad."

A frowning Killa Dre snatched the flyer from Banga's hand and looked it over. "Are you sure this is old girl?"

"Yeah, I'm sure that's that bitch! We're going there tonight, we're in that thang." Banga scowled. "Slide me to the house so I can get my strap."

"You sure you wanna go after this bitch tonight, though? I mean, you just got outta the hospital. I know those staples in your stomach are pretty fresh." Killa Dre reasoned, looking back and forth between the windshield and his homeboy.

"I may not run into this broad ever again." Banga said. "The opportunity has presented its self and I'm gonna take it. If you're not tryna ride then cool, but either way I'm getting down on this tonight."

Killa Dre nodded and said, "Alright, if this bitch gotta go tonight then she's gotta go. I'm with chu." He held out his fist. Banga looked to the fist then to his man before giving him a pound.

The rest of the ride to his apartment, Banga looked out of the window scowling, watching the streets pass him by in a blur.

Tonight was the night that his brother would finally be avenged.

$$$

Pavielle lay beside Vayda looking up at the black & white sonogram of his son. He couldn't be more excited about the bun baking in his fiancé's oven. He was sure that the birth of his son would be the happiest day of his life. He had a mental rolodex of possible names that he could give his baby boy, but he couldn't make up his mind.

"Yo, you see this?" Pavielle pointed to the baby's umbilical cord. "Is that my son's swipe?"

Vayda laughed and said, "No. That's not his dick, stupid! That's his umbilical cord."

"Hell naw, Blood, that's my baby's ding-a-ling." Pavielle took a closer look at the sonogram. "My lil' nigga got swipe just like his daddy."

"Boy, please." Vayda shook her head like he was silly.

Pavielle sat the sonogram on his chest and said, "That's brazy, Vay. I'm going to be a father. Some lil' boy is actually going to be calling me pop."

"I know, right? It all seems so surreal." She said. "I'm going to be a mother. I never thought the day would come, but here it is."

"Yeah, I just wish G-momma, my moms, and pops were here to celebrate lil' dude's homecoming with us." Pavielle picked up the portrait of his family from the dresser. He had glassy eyes that were attempting to form tears but he blinked them back.

"They are here, baby." Vayda told him as she stood to her knees behind him and wrapped her arms around his neck, pressing her cheek against his.

"In spirit, right?" Pavielle sat the portrait down on the dresser. "It's just not the same as being able to talk, touch, or feel a person in the flesh. There's a difference in seeing a person and imagining them there."

"I know, boo." Vayda said. "And I'm sorry that they can't be here in the physical to see our son when he's pushed out into this crazy, hectic world." She kissed him on the cheek and notice that his eyes were welling up with tears. If he were to blink tears would shoot down his cheeks. Suddenly, his cell phone rang and vibrated, dancing around on the dresser. He picked it up and pressed talk.

"What's up, duce owe?" Pavielle said into his cellular. Something was said on the line that made him look alive and sit up in bed. "Dre, get her to tell you where old boy is. Afterwards, y'all niggaz can cancel that bitch, peace."

He hung up.

$$$

Banga was in the corner of the club barely hidden within the shadows. He sat at his table babysitting a cranberry and vodka. He'd ordered the drink as to not look suspicious amongst other patrons in attendance. By no means was he considering indulging in alcohol that night. Nah, he needed a clear head if he was going to execute the mission at hand.

Banga had been at the club for the greater half of the night, so the ice cubes melted and mixed with his drink, watering it down. He played the background watching the scenery before him play out. Beautiful, scantily clad women moved about giving lap dances, serving drinks or dancing on the stage. The trick niggaz threw dollars in the air making it rain, while thirsty ass dudes tried to grab and grope the dancers. Banga had been offered several lap dances throughout the night, but he'd turned them all down, for fear of losing his concentration and missing Passion when she came out. He was at Club Mack Daddy that night on business, and it was that business alone that deserved his undivided attention.

Banga was just about to get up and look around to see if he'd see Passion around when he heard….

"Ladies and gentlemen…bitches and thirsty ass niggaz…get out your pocket books and wallets, and give a warm welcome to the amazing, the sensational, the dazzling, the oh so fine…Passion…" the DJ announced. Juicy J's *Bands will make her dance* came blasting from the speakers in the four upper corners of the club. Passion came walking out on stage like a horse. She was dressed in a chauffer's hat, black shades, a short tight fitting blazer and patent leather hooker boots that reached her thighs. She threw her hat into the audience and worked the pole for a bit before pulling off her blazer and tossing it aside. Bills of all denominations came falling out of the air and onto the stage.

Banga watched intently as his target performed. She was putting on one hell of a show. When he saw her the night she shot him and blasted on his brother she was dressed in all black and looked thugged out. But working the stage before him now she looked amazing, her body was worthy of the cover of Black Men Magazine. She was tantalizing and the way she moved seem to call out to him. Banga began imagining himself seven inches deep inside of Passion's pussy, giving her back strokes. The scene of him and her fucking played out in his mind like a hardcore porn flick. Just thinking about his cock sliding in and out of her coochie made his dick jump. Banga quickly shook the thought from his mind. This was the bitch that clapped him and smoked his brother. The only thing hard he was going to give her was a chest full of some hot shit.

Once Passion finished her performance, she and another stripper gathered up all of her earnings and stuffed them into three clear trash bags. It was the most money Banga had seen any of the girls make that night. He watched as Passion headed to the back to the locker room where all of the girls got dressed for their performances. He dropped a twenty on his table for the waitress and made to follow Passion. Confirming that she'd definitely went into the back room, Banga slipped outside and into the passenger seat of Killa Dre's Charger, where he was waiting behind the wheel.

"Blood, you look like Eazy E with that get-up on." Killa Dre laughed referring to the Jheri Curl wig, Oakland Raiders snapback and black shades Banga had worn as a disguise so that Passion wouldn't recognize him. "You see her in there?"

"Yeah, she should be coming out in a minute." Banga told him as he took off his disguise. He and Killa Dre watched the entrance of the club, paying close attention to everyone coming out. "There that hoe go, right there." Banga pointed to Passion who'd just emerged from the club with one of the bouncers following her to her car with the trash bags of money. Killa Dre waited a moment after she pulled off and followed behind her. They followed her all of the way home and parked across the street, two houses down from her residents. They watched her go into the house and close the door behind her.

Killa Dre slid his gloves on and pulled his burner from underneath his seat. "Alright, I'll be right back." He moved to open the door, but Banga grabbed his arm.

"She's mine; it was my brother that she peeled, if I let chu nod her it won't mean nothing." He gave him a stern look. Right after, he checked the magazine of his banger and chambering a round into its head.

Click! Clack!

Killa Dre nodded, understanding fully where his homeboy was coming from. Not too long ago he had tracked down his brother's murderer and spilled his blood. He couldn't imagine allowing someone else to take the vengeance that was meant for him. It was his brother; therefore it was his obligation to carry out the execution of his shooter.

"Hold it down; I'll be back in two shakes of a lamb's tail." Banga told him before hopping out of the car and jogging across the street, looking both ways.

$$$

The dining room glass table was completely covered with bills of all denominat-ions. Passion sat at the end of the table counting her take for the night by hand and occasionally taking sips from a glass of Amsterdam Vodka and Minute Maid fruit punch. Growing tired of counting, Passion sat the stack of money she'd been counting aside. She sat her purse on her lap and rummaged through it until she produced what she was looking for: a small zip-loc of heroin, a syringe, a tourniquet and a lighter. Passion went into the kitchen and got a spoon and a bottle of water. She emptied some of the heroin out onto the spoon along with some water. She struck a flame with her lighter and held it under the spoon until it heated and began to bubble. She then dropped a piece of cotton onto the spoon and allowed it to absorb the heroin. Seeing that the cotton had absorbed the heroin, Passion picked up the syringe and drew the heroin into it through the cotton. She sat the syringe down and picked up the tourniquet. She tied the tourniquet around her arm and pulled it tight with her teeth. Passion then smacked her arm until a green vein appeared before her eyes. Next, she picked up the syringe and penetrated her vein with the needle.

Passion had never considered doing heroin until she lost her best-friend and the love of her life. She and Traquila had known each other since junior high school. They lost their virginity together on the same night to the Kennedy twins and had their first experience with the same sex with one another. They were as tight as blood sisters, and even had one another's names tattooed on them. They'd even made a pact that when they'd died that they'd be buried right beside each other.

Losing Traquila was like losing a part of herself. Passion knew she'd never feel whole again. There was no one that could fill that void that Traquila left behind, so she looked for a temporary relief, and she found it in the form of heroin. One of the girls at the club had made the introductions between Passion and that boy heroin. At first she was hesitant to fuck with him, knowing how he got down and how he'd turned people out. But the retreat he provided from reality was too sweet to pass by, and before she knew it, Mr. H was snaking his way through her veins and into her heart. She had fallen in love, and what's worse is she became sprung. She found herself stalking him, trying to see him every day. And she did, but it came with a price, just like everything else that's worth having.

Once the needle broke the surface and entered Passion's vein, blood rushed inside of the syringe causing the heroin to look murky. She was just about to push the heroin into her vein when the lights went out in the house.

"Shit!" Passion cursed, removing the syringe from her arm and laying it on the table. She took a sip of her Vodka and fruit punch and walked over to the light switch. She flipped the light switch on and off, but it didn't come on. She heard the window over the kitchen sink shatter and it startled her, causing her to drop her glass of Vodka. The glass hit the floor and shattered into pieces, scattering shards everywhere. Passion ran for the front door, but tripped and fell on her side. Quickly, she got up on her feet and ran to the door. She undone all of the locks and removed the chain. As soon as she swung the door open her eyes lit up and she gasped.

Crack!

Banga smacked Passion across her head with the butt of his banger, spinning her around and dropping her to the floor.

"It's time to pay the piper, bitch!" he spoke with frightening eyes, stalking his way inside of the house with his gun at his side. Dazed and confused, Passion slowly got up on her knees and hands. "Yeah, big baby, it's about that time." Banga moved in to tie up the loose end, and suddenly she shot out of the living room, heading for the kitchen. Gritting his teeth, Banga gripped his cannon with both hands like One

Time and lifted it. He cracked off two rounds: one hit the kitchen doorway and sprayed splinters, while the other shattered a glass vase sitting on the windowpane.

Passion disappeared through the dooray.

"Shit." Banga fumed, pissed off that he'd missed his intended target. He crept into the kitchen with his burner raised at his shoulder; he peeked around the corner of the back porch doorway and was blinded by bleach to the eyes. He screamed as the liquid burned his sight, throwing an arm across his brows. Passion kicked him in the balls and he doubled over, grabbing his family jewels.

"Uhh!" She then tackled him. He hit the wall and his banger flew from his hand, hitting the floor and skidding across the surface in circles. While Banga lay on the floor grimacing and holding his testicles, he saw Passion running for his banger and he stuck his foot out. She tripped over his leg and went crashing to the floor, bumping her head. Banga scrambled to his feet and turned on the faucet. He cupped his hands under the flowing water and washed out his eyes as best as he could. He used his shirt to dry his eyes and moved to get his banger, which was lying beside a dazed Passion. While Banga had been drying his eyes with his shirt, Passion saw the stitches and staples in his torso from his surgery. Seeing him reaching for his weapon, she snarled like a wild tigress and drove her arcylic nails into the wedges of his stitches. Banga's eyes bugged and he screamed in agony, he'd never felt such a searing excruciation. Passion gritted her teeth and gave him an evil glare. She dug her nails further in between his stitches, reopening his wound and spilling his blood. Banga dropped to his knees; he was in so much pain that he couldn't even scream anymore. Passion's fingers were halfway into his wound and she was forcing them in even deeper. The hoodlum was paralyzed by her attack, but he had to do something before she managed to kill him. With that in mind, Banga balled his fist tight and cracked her ass across the jaw, laying her the fuck out. Leaking all over the place, Banga held his stomach and crawled toward his joint. Passion moaned as she lay on the floor trying to gather her wits. Banga scooped his weapon into his palm and wrapped his finger around the trigger. He went to turn around and felt a sharp pain at the top of his shoulder that caused him to holler out. He brought himself around and saw Passion with a crazed look in her eyes about to bring a butcher's knife down again.

Blam!

A bullet ripped through Passion's shoulder and she hit the floor, dropping the butcher's knife. It clasped when it hit the linoleum. She clenched her jaws tightly, trying to fight the fire in her shoulder. She looked to her right and saw the butcher's knife lying two feet from her grasp. It was shiny and stained with her victim's blood. With her sights set on it, she went to grab it and a gaping hole appeared on her thigh. She hollered and grabbed her thigh, having been shot.

"Youz about a hard headed ass bitch," Killa Dre shook his head pitifully. He saw Passion look to the butcher's knife again. "You wanna try going for it again? Go ahead. The next shot will put chu in a sleep so deep nobody will be able to wake you up from it." Seeing that homegirl wasn't about to test his gangsta, Killa Dre glanced at Banga. "You all right, Blood?" He asked his homeboy. Not waiting for an answer, Killa Dre kept his gun trained on Passion while he lifted

Banga's shirt. What he saw made him cringe and lower the shirt. "Hold on, B. We're going to get chu some help, dawg." He assured his comrade and walked over to the stripper.

"Where is that nigga Paybacc hiding at?" Killa Dre asked watching Passion bawl on the floor, wincing. She was in a world of pain and didn't answer him. Killa Dre blew hard and kneeled down. He clutched her jaws causing her mouth to open and stuck his banger into it, making her gag on the gun's metal. "I'ma run this by you one more time, sweetheart. Where the fuck is Paybacc?" he asked with a no nonsense attitude. Tears ran from the corners of Passion's eyes as she tried to say something with a mouth full of metal. Killa Dre took the gun from out of her mouth and listened to what she had to say. She gasped for air for a time, before taking a deep breath to speak.

"Suck my pussy, mothafucka! I'm not telling you shit, so you may as well kill me now." She barked as she glared up at his young ass. There was no way she was offering up the man she loved. Fuck that, bitches like her were built Ford tough. She'd already lost Traquila and she wasn't about to lose

Paybacc. Nah, she wouldn't tell Killa Dre Paybacc's whereabouts even if it meant her life.

Killa Dre punched Passion across the chin and knocked her out cold. He then pulled off his belt and Banga's belt. He sat his banger on Passion's chest and used the belts to bind her wrists and ankles.

"Agh, fuck," Banga cursed as he used the kitchen table to pull himself to his feet on wobbily legs. He staggered to the wall and leaned against it. He was holding his stomach and Killa Dre could see his white T-shirt soaked in his blood. He looked to be suffering as a result of Passion reopening the wound that was held together by stitches and staples. "See…See if you can find a stapler, Blood, hurry up." He urged him, the pain he was experiencing etched across his face.

Killa Dre looked around the house until he found a staple-gun. Banga told him what he wanted to him to do and he nodded in understanding. Banga held his wound closed and Killa Dre stapled his middle back up. With each staple that penetrated his hide, the hoodlum winced. Once Killa Dre was done, Banga moved him aside and picked his banger back up. He approached Passion and leveled his banger with her dome.

"Stall her out for now, B. We're going to torture that whore 'til she tells us where Paybacc is laying low." Killa Dre told him as he gripped his shoulder. "After that, you're free to do away with her." Once Banga obliged him, he tossed him the car keys. "Bring the car around into the backyard, I'ma be taking her out."

$$$

Pavielle, Gangsta and Gouch stood out on the front porch of his house politicking and rotating a blunt amongst them. The gate of the driveway was open while the Muslims patrolled the grounds. Pavielle had gotten a call from Killa Dre saying that the hit had gone horribly wrong and that Banga had been seriously injured. He told him that he was gunning it to his house and for him to have the gate open.

Gangsta took a glance at his watch and turned to Pavielle. "It's one o'clock now, what time did Dre call you?"

"About twenty-five or thirty minutes ago," Pavielle said, smoking a cigarette.

"They should have been here," Gouch stated. "You think something happened along the way?"

"Shit, I hope not." Pavielle blew smoke and then flicked the cigarette butt, sending embers flying.

"That fool Banga wild as a mothafucka. My young hitta putting it down and he just got outta. Stomach all stapled up and shit. He didn't even take a break to heal up." Gouch shook his head sadly.

"Look at it this way, had it been me or your brother that this bitch bodied, would you be looking to rest up before you went looking for her, or would you be trying to pop her as soon as you got the chance?" Gangsta gave him a look as serious as cancer.

Gouch thought on it for a time. Had it been Gangsta or Pavielle that Passion had killed, he'd be out looking for that bitch day and night; from sun up to sun down. There was no doubt about that. If he didn't have any hands to bust his guns, or feet to kick her ass, and he was just a head, he'd be trying to bite on her ankles until she bled to death.

Gangsta saw the look in his nephew's eyes and knew what his answer would be.

"You feel me?" Gangsta rested his arm on his shoulder.

Gouch nodded.

The sound of screeching tires cut through the night as a black Dodge Charger bent the corner and barreled down the residential block as if it were in a high speed chase. It entered the driveway of Pavielle's home and headed to the backyard. The Muslims quickly closed and locked the gate back. Pavielle stepped off the porch telling Nasheed and his men to continue to hold down the fort.

Killa Dre hopped out of the Charger and ran around to the passenger side. He pulled the door open and to assist his homeboy. He pulled Banga's arm over his shoulder and helped him step out of the car. Banga wasn't bleeding as bad as he once was, but he was still in great pain and needed medical attention.

"Come on, man, we gotta get chu into the house." Killa Dre told him, looking at his wincing face and hearing his groans of pain.

"Holy shit, was he shot?" Pavielle asked as he, Gangsta and Gouch came into the backyard.

"Nah, that bitch reopened his wound from his surgery." Killa Dre informed them.

Gouch ran over to Banga and threw his arm over his shoulder. He and Killa Dre helped him toward the back porch door. "I'll help you get'em inside and then I'll call the Doc."

"The Doc?" Killa Dre's forehead wrinkled.

"Yeah, he's an older homie from the set. He turned his life around and went to medical school." Gouch told him of one of the most successful homies from their set. "He'll know just what to do."

"Homegirl is in the trunk." Killa Dre put Gangsta in the know.

Once Killa Dre and Gouch had helped Banga inside of the house, Gangsta reached inside of the driver side window and activated the button that popped the trunk. He then approached the trunk with Pavielle by his side.

"This broad is the key to finding Paybacc and ending this madness." Gangsta told his youngest nephew before he opened the trunk. Holding the trunk open, he saw Passion lying on her side with her wrists and ankles bonded by belts. He pulled her over onto her back. Her eyes were staring at nothing and her mouth was stuffed with a gag.Upon further inspection, he discovered the blood that coated the inside of the trunk. "Oh, no, don't fucking tell me! Don't fucking tell me!" he ripped the duct-tape from Passion's mouth and removed the sock, tossing it aside. He slapped Passion in the face as if he were trying to wake her up. Still, she lay motionless with lifeless eyes. Gangsta tried performing CPR on her to bring her back, but his efforts were to

no avail. "Fuck!" he cursed, kicking the fender and back tire of the Charger in a mothafucking tantrum. Exhausted, he sat on the ground and leaned back against the fender, clutching his head with both hands. "I don't know what we're going to do now; this bitch was our only lead to Paybacc."

Chapter Ten

The next day

Paybacc sat on the couch rotating metal Chinese therapy balls in his palm as he stared aimlessy, listening to what Domino was telling him.

"Why don't chu say something, cuz? You're just sitting there looking spaced out and shit." Domino stated from where he sat on the kitchen table.

"What do you want me to say, Loco? Paybacc replied never breaking his stare, or stopping the rotating of the Chinese therapy balls in his palm. "It's a cold world, you gotta keep your heater with chu, feel me? I'm not even surprised. I had a feeling that there was a flaw in playboy's character, but since he was your protégé I pushed that thought to the back of my mental. I have been neglecting this situation long enough; the time has come for me to address it."

"What do you think we should do?" Domino asked. Paybacc shot Domino a look that caused him to hang his head. He'd seen that look on his mentor's face enough times to know that it meant the streets would be claiming another lost soul. He looked back up at his big homie with glassy eyes and said, "Alright, I brought him into the fold, so I'll do the deed?"

"I'ma bastard, but I'm not a heartless one, at least not when it comes to my niggaz. Nah, I wouldn't ask you to get your hands dirty. Wacko's life is mine to claim, rest at ease." Paybacc said to Domino, hoping his words put his little homie at ease.

"I know I shouldn't ask, considering the nature of the situation and with it being your life that was hanging in the balance, but can you make it quick and clean?" Domino asked of Wacko's execution.

Paybacc thought on it as he massaged his chin and said, "Normally, I'd make this a dirty and slow death, but since my lil' homie is asking...OK." he nodded. Domino closed his eyes and blew hard, relieved that his big homie was going to give his young protégé a merciful death. "I'll make it quick, one through the back of the melon, he won't feel a thing."

"Thanks, cuz."

"Don't wet it, we're family."

A knock at the door silenced the living room. Domino hopped off of the kitchen table and approached the door. "Who is it?" he asked gripping his burner, which was still tucked inside his waistline.

"Turbo," a voice answered from the other side of the door. Domino took a quick glance through the curtains, confirming who it was. He looked back at Paybacc and he gave a nod. He then opened the door and allowed a man inside that was built to play on the defensive line for the Pitsburg Steelers. He rocked a meaty shaved head and walked with a slight limp thanks to his bum leg. Turbo slapped hands with Domino as he crossed the threshold into Paybacc's home. He removed his striped Orlando Magics snapback and stood before the man that he'd come to see, fidgeting with it.

"Are you still offering those five stacks for information on the whereabouts of that redbone of Booby Loco's?" Turbo asked timidy. The nigga look like a mothafucking slave scared to look his master in the eyes as he asked for something.

Staring into Turbo's eyes, Paybacc could see that he'd subcummed to the allure of crack cocaine. His face looked dry and ashy and his bottom jaw was biting to the side. The signs were there. On top of that, Turbo was avoiding eye contact which let him know that he was ashamed for Payabcc to see him in his current state. Looking at Turbo, Paybacc couldn't help but think how the mighty had fallen. Before he had gotten locked up, Turbo was slinging and getting his slice of the American pie. Now he was a shell of his former shelf. Crack had really did a number on him.

Paybacc nodded. "The offer is still on the table, homie."

"Well, uh, I know where she's staying."

This made Paybacc put the metal Chinese balls down on the coffee-table and sit up. Turbo now had his undivided attention.

"Where?" Paybacc could see that Turbo was leery about telling him where Vayda was without getting paid first, so he dipped into his pocket. He pulled out a wad of money and quickly counted through it. "This is twenty-seven hundred dollars." He tossed the bills on the table. "You'll get the rest once you tell me where this bitch is."

"I gotta address, I wrote it down." Turbo pulled a piece of paper from out of his back pocket and handed it to Paybacc. He continued to talk as Paybacc looked the address over. "I saw redbone coming home one day; she and the boy Booby. I was across the street cutting Mr. Johnson's yard when they rolled up. As soon as they drove up into the driveway, about four or five brothers in suits swarmed the car, helping her get out bags and stuff. From their attire they had to be Muslims.They're always there. I think they guard the place or something."

Paybacc nodded and said, "I know exactly where this is. Good looking." Turbo picked up the money from the coffee-table and Paybacc ushered him toward the door. "You know Rocko, right?" Turbo nodded. "Go see him. He's at the trap over there on 45th; he'll take care of you. I'll let'em know that you're coming. Oh, and, uh, Turbo," Turbo looked to Paybacc. "If I find out you fucked me on this, I'm going to come see you...personally." He stared the crackhead dead in his eyes wearing a serious expression. He knew that a fiend would do or say anything to get a fix. And even though he knew the nigga fairly well, his loyalty to crack was greater than his loyalty to him.

"Ah, nah, cuz, this is square business," Turbo assured him. "You'll see for yourself."

Paybacc nodded and closed the door behind Turbo. He looked to Domino with a shit-eating-grin and he returned the gesture.

It was time to kill the head so that the body will fall.

Chapter Eleven

It was two o'clock in the evening and the sun was out in full bloom, warming the once cold streets with its rays and spreading light throughout the ghetto. The sight of the sun was The Children of the Night's cue to take it in, while it was the working class sign to head out for their respective destinations.

McArthur Park was alive with children running around laughing and playing under the watchful eyes of their parents. Creeper pushed his kid sister, Arlene, on the swing as she giggled and smiled. Creeper wore a smirk on his face as he watched his sister enjoy herself. Seeing her happy was like therapy for him. He was so wrapped up in the moment that he had temporarily forgotten about the ills of his reality.

"Higher, Ruben, higher," Arlene cooed.

"Alright, you asked for it." Creeper pushed Arlene harder in the swing.

"Weeee," Arlene said as her brother pushed her swing further into the air, her hair wafting at her rear and her feet sticking out in front of her. "Push faster, harder, Ruben!"

"If I push any faster or harder, you're going to go flying into orbit." Creeper warned her with a smirk on his lips. Looking up, he saw Gangsta, Pavielle, Gouch and Killa Dre hop out of a black Mercedes Benz and move in his direction. "They're here." Creeper looked back at Black Jesus who was posted under a tree with Bullet by his side. He'd been there smoking his Cuban cigar and watching Creeper interact with his kid sister. Bullet was parlaying on the table chopping it up with some one in Spanish about business. Once Black Jesus tapped him and pointed in Gangsta and company's direction, Bullet told whoever he was talking to he had to go and put his cell on his waistline.

"Watch Arlene," Black Jesus told Bullet. Bullet hopped off of the table and went to do as his brother commanded. He took over for Creeper, pushing his sister in the swing.

"I'll be back, mija." Creeper told Arlene and went to meet Gangsta.

Gangsta exchanged pleasantries with everyone and introduced Creeper to Gouch and Pavielle. Creeper, Gouch and Pavielle threw their heads back like "What's up?" and slapped hand s with the Vato.

"So, what's the reason behind this hush, hush meeting?" Gangsta asked Black Jesus as he buttoned his suit's jacket.

"Your boy Paybacc…I'm his supplier." Creeper informed Gangsta.

"How do you know we got funk with'em?" Gangsta's brows furrowed.

"Creeper and I have a rapport." Black Jesus interjected. "Naturally this enemy of yours name came up. That's not all either. You guys may have an enemy in common. You know, Arsenegger? That crooked detective that's been riding you like a wild bronco? Well, Creeper seems to think he murdered his brother."

"I can tell you right now, that D is as dirty as they come. I wouldn't put it past him." Gangsta stated seriously. "Now back to Paybacc, how'd you come into contact with him?"

"Through a customer of mine, he goes by the name of Domino." Creeper told him.

"Domino from Eastside Crips?" Pavielle asked from behind black sunglasses. The sun bounced off the side of them and birthed a sparkle.

"Yeah, that's him. He brought him to me." Creeper confirmed.

"Do you know where we can find this mothafucka?" Gouch asked.

Creeper shook his head and said, "No. But I am supposed to meet him for a re-up around seven o'clock tonight." He glanced at the presidential Rolex that adorned his wrist.

"Where at?" Gangsta inquired, folding his arms to his chest. He appeared to be visibly interested in what Creeper had to say.

Creeper told him the address where he was to meet Paybacc to re-up. The Vato's forehead wrinkled once he saw that Gangsta wasn't writing anything down. "Don't chu think you should be writing this down?" he asked.

"It's all upstairs." Gangsta pointed to his temple. "Listen, I appreciate chu hitting us with this info. I'm sure you have an idea of what's going to happen once we get ahold of this cat. That means you're going to be losing out on business, so why lead this dude to a slaughter? What's in it for you? What do you want?"

"I'm doing this outta love for Jesus and Bullet, they're my brothers." Creeper told him. "They say you're a standup guy, I could always use one of those in my circle. All I want outta this is your friendship." He extended his hand and Gangsta shook it. "There's one more thing."

"Ahhh, the catch, there's always one. What is it?" Gangsta smirked.

"Arsenegger…he's mine." Creeper said with fierceness in his eyes.

"You got that." Gangsta slapped hands with him and embraced him.

The deal was chiseled in stone.

That night

Banga sat up in bed peering up at Killa Dre through hooded eyes. He was so high off of morphine that he could barely make heads or tails of where he was or who he was talking to. The night before the Doc had come out to Pavielle's home re-stitched, stapled, and bandaged his wound. Now he lay in bed with his lady to take care of him.

Killa Dre snapped his fingers and waved his hand before Banga's eyes. "Are you here with me, Blood? How many fingers am I holding up?" he held up the middle-finger.

Banga laughed and said, "Old funny ass dude."

Killa Dre smiled. "Man, you're so shit faced right now."

"Yeahhhhhh, buddy, this morphine is something…something wonderful." Bang smiled happily. "I haven't felt this good since…since…shit, a nigga ain't never felt this good." He chuckled.

"Don't go turning junkie on me now."

"Nah, never that, I done seen what drugs do to people, fam. How stupid would I be to fall victim to some shit that I know is bad for me?"

"I feel you, but how many niggaz know what drugs do to people, but still choose to Tango with addiction?"

"True that." Banga agreed. "We're all dogs, but I'ma different breed."

"Two sho'," Killa Dre nodded and glanced at his G-shock. "Well, look I gotta go. I'll come back to check on you once I take care of this business."

"You know I'm nosy, right? What business?"

Killa Dre leaned closer. "You know old boy that hit the trap with them broads? Well, we've gotta lead on dude, got it setup so he'll come right to us."

"Blood is a part of the crew that set it off on me, baby bro and Monk." Banga said, hearing the name of the cat that orchestrated the hit on he and his brother damn near made him sober up. "Peanut, get my guns!" he yelled out to his girlfriend. When he threw the covers from his person and tried to get up, but pain shot through his stomach. He grimaced and Killa Dre helped him back in bed.

"You're in no shape to put in work." Killa Dre covered Banga back up. "Get yourself some rest; me and the homies can handle this."

"Alright," Banga nodded. He was too weak to put up a fight. "You just make sure you put a couple hot ones in that son of a bitch in honor of baby bro and Monk."

Killa Dre gave Banga a nod then grasped his hand firmly in a display of love and comradery. "I'm up." The young nigga rose from his iron-chair and left the bedroom.

$$$

"So, where this pussy at?" Wacko asked from the backseat. His head was beneath a hood and his eyes were behind black sunglasses. His hand was wrapped up in a blue bandana, which concealed the banger he was clutching. He was ready to add another body to his resume.

"42nd and Halldale, we're almost there." Paybacc said from the passenger seat where he was taking pulls from a blunt and exhausting smoke. He had a black beanie pulled over his brows and his hulking frame filled out a black sweatshirt.

"What's up with you, cuz? You haven't said shit the whole ride." Wacko asked Domino as he took the blunt from Paybacc.

Domino looked up at Wacko through the rearview and shook his head. "I'm good. Just thinking on how this nigga ran off with this dough, fronting on the team like we're soft or something. Shit really got me heated, cuz."

Wacko nodded and blew smoke from his nose. "I feel you, Loc. But once I slump this chump the rest of these niggaz are gonna get the message loud and clear: don't fuck with us. So, don't wet this shit. Sit back, relax, and bare witness to my G."

Wacko's appetite for ghetto stardom would be his undoing. Paybacc had cooked up a story about some cat robbing one of his stash houses and making off with a hundred racks. He told the little nigga that he knew exactly where the dude was, knowing that the youth was hungry to earn a reputation and would be down to put in the work.

Paybacc and Domino were driving Wacko out to a crack head's house that they'd rented out. Payback would allow Wacko to enter the house first then come in behind him to put one in the back of his skull, ending his life.

Paybacc's cell phone rang and he answered it.

"What's cracking?" he spoke into his cellular. "I actually had something on the line. What's with the time change? Six?" he glanced at the clock on his cell phone. "Shit, that's thirty minutes from now. Short ass notice; alright, fuck it. Peace." He hung up and looked to Domino. "Turn this bitch around, Creeper moved the meeting up."

"For what?" Domino asked as he busted a U-turn.

Paybacc shrugged. "All he said was that something came up, so I don't know. I already got the dough in the trunk, so just slide to the address. You remember it?"

Domino nodded yes.

"Ah, cuz, I thought I was about to go split me a nigga." Wacko stated disappoint-ed and set back in the seat.

"Oh, nah, that business is getting handled tonight, so I hope you're still in killa mode then." Paybacc looked to the backseat.

"I'm always in killa mode, cuz." Wacko assured him.

$$$

"He should be here any minute now." Creeper glanced at his Rolex while his other hand gripped a 12 gauge shotgun. He was standing in the far right corner of the living room of the condemned house.

"How many are coming in?" Gouch asked from the far left corner, holding an AK-47 with an extended banana clip. His trigger finger was itching to give a squeeze and catch a body.

"Three. But he may come in alone." Creeper told him.

"You all right, Dre?" Gangsta asked Killa Dre from where he stood in the top left corner, his hand wrapped around a Tec-9.

"I'm two-hundred; I can't wait to do this nigga and get'em outta our hair." Killa Dre said from the top right corner both hands gripping an Uzi with the extender on the barrel.

"I can't either. Booby's gonna text me once he sees them pull up. Just be ready." Gangsta told him.

It was almost that time.

$$$

Domino turned on the block that their destination was on. He coasted through the avenue looking for the address.

Paybacc tapped Domino's arm and said, "I think that's it coming up. The peanut butter colored stucco house with the boarded up windows."

"Mothafucka looks spookier than a bitch." Wacko said, peering out the backseat window at the house.

"Hell yeah, looks like Freddy Kruger lives there." Domino commented, pulling over to the side of the curb across the street from the house.

Paybacc narrowed his eyes into slits once he saw someone poke their head up from over the dashboard of an H2 Hummer. He didn't know if he was tripping out from being high, or was he actually being spyed on. He shook the thought from his head, reasoning that the weed was making him paranoid.

$$$

"He's here!" Gangsta announced to everyone else as he glanced at the screen of his cell phone after it vibrated on his waistline. The announcement made everyone prepare themselves for the task at hand. Their fingers settled on the triggers of their respective weapons ready to give a squeeze and turn someone into a human cheese grater. Gangsta put his finger to his lips for the silence of his comrades once he heard the doorknob of the front door twist and turn as it was being fondled. The door swung open and the streetlights outlined the silhouette of the man standing in the doorway. The man peered through the darkness making out the figures in the far corners of the living room.

"What the…" The man managed to get out before his ears were filled with gunfire. He did a funny dance on his feet as slugs hit him from every angle imaginable. Once the gunfire ceased, the man tipped over and hit the floor, face first. The blood from his form slowly began to outline his form as he lay twisted.

Gangsta rushed over to the slain man with everyone else surrounding him. He grabbed the man by his shoulder and pulled him over onto his back. The man's face was bloody. Gaping holes covered his face and his eye had been blown out by a bullet. His one good eye was wide open and his mouth was agap. The man wasn't Paybacc, but his face registered in Gangsta's mental. It was Wacko from Eastside Crips.

"This isn't him!" Gangsta announced to his comrades. At that precise moment, the sound of screeching tires filled the air followed by gunfire. Gangsta and company ran outside ready to join the firefight.

$$$

"What chu looking at, cuz?" Domino asked Paybacc. He followed his line of vision and found a Hummer at the end of it. He studied the Hummer but didn't see anything out of place.

Paybacc shook his head and said, "Nothing, cuz. Mothafucking weed got me paranoid." He brought his hand down his face and blew hard. He thought he saw another flicker of movement inside the Hummer but paid it no mind. "Yo, Wack, make that exchange for me, Loco. The dough is in that duffle bag in the hatch underneath the sparetire."

"You won't me to go in there?" His face balled up as he pointed to the stuccoed house.

"Yeah, cuz, I know lil' Wacko from The Bottoms ain't scared? I know he ain't." Paybacc asked playing on his little homie's ego.

"Never that," Wacko retorted. He grabbed the duffle bag from the hatch of the Yukon and hopped out of the truck. Domino and Paybacc watched as he jogged across the street and into the yard of the house. He knocked first then turned the knob. They watched as he stepped through the door. For a moment there was silence then gunfire erupted, and Wacko went down in a roar of gun smoke.

Domino grabbed his heater and went to hop out, but Paybacc grabbed his arm saying, "Nigga, are you crazy? Get the fuck outta here! That nigga's gone." Domino resurrected the Yukon and screeched away from the curb. "Pull upon that Hummer, cuz!" Paybacc comman-ded as he pulled his Tec-9 from under the passenger seat. Once Domino pulled upon the side of the Hummer, he put his arm to his chest for him to lay back. He brought his Tec-9 around with the other hand, pointing it at the driver side window of the Hummer and pulling the trigger. The Tec vibrated in Paybacc's palm as it cut loose, igniting its muzzle. He pulled his smoking weapon back seeing that he'd only left scratches behind on the driver side window of the vehicle.

Suddenly, the back window of the Yukon exploded as bullets passed through it. Domino floored it away from the scene. Paybacc snuck a peek over the headrest. He saw Pavielle in the middle of the street discharging his burner in their direction.

Paybacc laughed and said, "Fucking faggot! These niggaz can't catch The Locsta, cuz." He turned around back in his seat. Domino glanced at him, but kept on mashing through the residential block through stop signs.

$$$

Pavielle lowered his .9mm automatic to his side as it wafted with smoke. He stared at the back lights of the Yukon until it disappeared down the block and into the darkness.

Gangsta, Gouch, Killa Dre and Creeper ran out into the street to his aide, but it was already too late.

"You get'em?" Gangsta looked to Pavielle.

Pavielle shook his head regretfully and said, "No. Let's get outta here before Binem turn out."

Chapter Twelve

Domino sat on the couch with a sniper rifle lying across his legs. He cleaned the scope of the rifle with a blue bandana and occasionally brushed the top of his head with his palm. It was something he did whenever he had something on his mind that was bugging him. Domino's eyes held a glassy look to them and he seemed to be hurt about something. He lay back on the couch and watched Paybacc toss bands of wrinkled bills into a duffle bag. A burning cigarette dangled from the corner of his full lips as he went about his business.

"I'm telling you, Loco, L.A is smaller than a mothafucka." Paybacc stated, ashes dropping from the end of his cigarette. "Everybody knows everybody out this bitch. Who would have thought our plug had ties with that nigga Gangsta? They almost got me up outta here. If it wasn't for Wacko biting the bullet I would have been a goner."

"Them niggaz got the lil' homie, cuz. Fuck!" Domino cursed, hating to have lost Wacko. "We should have hopped outta the joint and gave them boys that work."

Paybacc snatched the cigarette out of his mouth. "Fuck you talking about? That nigga was gone get it either way, this way his lil' bitch ass served a purpose. Sheeeiiit, lil' punk mothafucka was gone try to take me out? Cuz, fuck him and whoever else feel some type of way about'em being gone." He stared at Domino while taking pulls of his cigarette. His face fixed with a scowl.

"He wasn't supposed to go out that way. Cuz suffered. You were going to make sure it was quick and clean." Domino reasoned. "The slobs done'em up though. He'll be lucky if he gets an opened casket funeral."

"I'll be damned if I sit here and grieve over a nigga that was gone knock me over. Fuck I look like?" Paybacc asked rhetorically.

"I'm just saying he shouldn't have gone out like that."

Paybacc narrowed his eyes into slits at Domino. He switched hands with the cigarette and whipped out his Tec-9, pointing it in his direction. Domino was startled and caught off guard. His eyes grew big and his mouth shot open. He knew if he even attempted to move that Paybacc would unload on his monkey ass.

"What chu saying, cuz? Would you have rather it been me that walked through that door?" Paybacc barked angrily with his finger settled on the trigger of the Tec-9. He loved Domino like he'd skeeted him from his dick, but he'd kill him dead if he thought he felt it should have been him that ended up riddled with bullets and lying a bloody mess instead of Wacko. It would kill him to peel Domino's cap, but he couldn't afford to have any weak links in the chain of his organization. Anybody against him had to go, there were no exemptions.

"Nah, cuz, that's not what I'm saying." Domino assured him. "If I felt that way he would be here instead of you. I could have been a snake and went along with Wacko. We could have pushed you and took over the operation, but I kept it G like I'm supposed to. I told him like I'm telling you; I know where my loyalty lies." He stared his big homie dead in his eyes. He wasn't afraid of dying, so if he squeezed that trigger he'd embraced death like a relative at a family reunion.

Paybacc had taught him to fear nothing and no one, not even death it self.

Paybacc sat his Tec-9 on top of the stereo and continued tossing the bands into the duffle bag. "I don't wanna hear anymore about Wacko; tonight was the end of his chapter. I'll pay for his funeral and lay some paper on his peoples, but that's it. From now on it's me and you. It's up to us to keep this shit moving, cuz. Feel me?" Domino nodded. "I love you, man. You're my son." He grabbed Domino by the back of the neck and pulled him close, kissing him on top of the head.

"I love you, too."

"Come on, let's raise up outta here." Paybacc slung the duffle bag over his shoulder and waved him on.

Later that night

Paybacc watched his daughter dance around her bedroom as she went about the task of cleaning it. As Zora vacuumed, he imagined her growing up before his eyes. She went from six years old to eighteen years old. A rare smile emerged upon Paybacc's five o'clock shadowed face. It was at that moment that he regretted spending the past thirteen years of her life locked behind bars. He had missed the best part about being a parent, and that was watching your child grow up. If he could press rewind on his life, the bullets that entered the cop he'd shot would go back into his gun, the gun would go back on his waistline, and he'd be spending that night at his baby momma's house playing with little Zora. He wished his life had a rewind button, but it didn't. Therefore, he had to finish living out his life and playing the hand that fate had dealt him.

Paybacc knocked on his daughter's bedroom window. Zora turned off the vacuum and cautiously approached her bedroom window. She pulled the curtain back and smiled when she saw her father. Paybacc smiled back and pointed toward the front door. Zora nodded yes and left her bedroom. Paybacc stepped upon the porch, looking over his shoulder as he waited for Zora to come to the door. The whole time he kept his thumb hooked in the loop of his Levi's 501's right beneath the heater on his waistline. Although Zora and her mother lived in a quiet suburb of Los Angeles, taking precautions was a must. He had a fifty thousand dollar bounty on his head, and he knew a couple of head busters wouldn't mind traveling a little distance to collect the bread on him. He knew that fifty grand may as well had been $500,000 dollars in this economy.

Hearing the door coming unchained and the locks coming undone brought Paybacc's attention to the front door. The door pulled open and Zora stood before him smiling from ear to ear.

"Come in." she waved him inside.

Paybacc shook his head. "Nah, I can't stay."

Zora pulled the door closed and stepped out onto the porch. She kissed her father on the cheek and embraced him. "How are you?"

"I'm good, how about chu?"

"I'm straight." She told him. "It's pretty cold out here, are you sure you don't wanna come inside?"

"This isn't a social call, baby. I just came to drop you off something." He handed her a duffle bag. She peered inside and her eyes lit up. "That's two-hundred large. That's way more than enough to pay for school and buy your self a car. You can play with the rest."

"Daddy, what am I going to do with all of this money?" Zora asked.

"Exactly what I just told you to do." Paybacc answered. "Put that up as soon as you go back inside. You don't want your mother finding out you have it 'cause she'll never let chu keep it. She knows how I'm getting it out in these streets and will only see it as blood money."

"OK." Zora slung the duffle bag over her shoulder. She noticed her father looking over his shoulder for the third time since she'd stepped outside. Sensing that something was wrong, her stomach dropped and she wondered what kind of trouble he'd gotten into this time. "Is everything all right? Is someone after you? Is it because of this money?"

"Nah, your daddy earned that paper, every dollar of it. It's mine and I'm giving it to you." He looked her in the eyes.

"Then why do you keep looking over your shoulder?"

"I gotta situation, but it's nothing a beast can't handle." Paybacc smacked his hand over his heart. "These streets are a safari and I'm a lion; the most feared and ferocious animal of them all. That's how you gotta be if you ever gonna have a chance of surviving out here." Zora's eyes welled up with tears as she stared into her father's eyes. She was terrified that something was going to happen to him. After thirteen years she'd finally gotten him back. The last thing she wanted was for him to be taken away from her forever. "Why are you crying?" he asked, wiping her tears away with his fingers.

"I've just gotten you back; I don't wanna lose you again." Zora's voice cracked with emotion.

"Aww, baby, nothing is gonna happen to me." Paybacc embraced his daughter lovingly. She hugged him with her free arm and allowed the tears to flow freely down her face. Paybacc tried to break his embrace but she held fast, not wanting to let him go. She thought that she'd never be able to hold her father again and wanted to prolong the moment. "I gotta go, Zo."

"OK." She replied, kissing him on the side of his face. "I love you, dad." She yelled out to him as he walked over to his Chrysler 300.

"I love you too, baby." He yelled back.

"I'ma pray for you." She replied, wiping the tears from her face.

"Don't pray for your daddy, baby. Pray for these fuck-niggaz out here tryna get one up on me." He hopped into his whip and drove off.

Chapter Thirteen

Detective Dupri stood behind his wife with his hands gripping her hips as she chopped up cucumbers for a salad. He placed soft kisses up the side of her neck and nibbled on her ear, causing her nipples to harden and her to smile.

"Come on, baby, I'm tryna get dinner ready and you playing with my spot." Mrs. Dupri told him. Her mouth was saying no, but her body was saying yes. She let go of a soft moan as she felt her husband's bulge against her ample butt, grinding into her. "Come on now, Jeremiah's here."

"Let me get a little taste, I promise I'll be quick." He whispered into her ear as he licked up her neck and slid her panties down around her thighs. He already had his zipper undone and his meat was sticking out through the opening. He was so hard that veins were running all through his rod and his dick head was pulsating, precum dripped from the tip of it.

Dupri took a hold of his cock, using his thumb he attempted to guide his staff into his wife's wet, pinkness as she hiked her ass up for him.

"Daddy, Uncle Ryan's on TV!" young Jerimiah said from the doorway of the kitchen, startling his mother and father. They quickly fixed their clothes and tried to act natural, but it was too late. "What're you guys doing?" he asked curiously. His forehead creased with a line.

"Nothing," Dupri zipped his pants up and ate a cucumber.

"Unh unh, y'all were finna hump." Young Jeremiah called his father on his lie.

"Boy, what chu know about humping somebody." Dupri threw a sliced cucumber at his son, causing him to laugh and giggle. "Now, who did you say was on the tube?"

"Uncle Ryan. Come look." Young Jerimiah grabbed his father by the hand and led him into the living room, his mother followed behind.

Dupri and his wife sat down on the couch with young Jerimiah sitting between them. They stared intently at the TV screen at the broadcast that playing before them.

Detective Ryan Arsenegger was captured on camera gunning down Mira Ramirez and Luis Santos. In what was at first believed to be a justifiable homicide has now been confirmed as cold blooded murder, thanks to a video-tape that has been sent in anonymously...

Dupri watched the rest of the broadcast before hurrying down into the basement and recovering his burn-out cell phone. He took the sim chip out of the cell phone on his waistline and added it to the cell phone he had stashed. He turned the cell on, scrolled through the contacts until he found the number he was looking for, and pressed send. The line rang twice before Detective Maza answered.

"Aye, you see the news?"

"Yeah, I'm still watching it, the shits on every channel." Maza replied already knowing what Dupri was talking about. He was just about to call Dupri but he'd beaten him to it.

"This is bad, Maza, this is really fucking bad." Dupri said, rubbing his bald head. "These guys know a lotta shit about us, they have more than enough dirt to bury us alive."

"What're you talking about?" Maza asked. "It's those two assholes that got caught popping a couple of kids. What does this have to do with us?"

"Bargaining chips, they may sing like The Temptations for a lighter sentence."

"How do you even know that they'll say anything?"

"I don't, and neither do you, so why take a chance? Let's nip this problem in the bud before it manifests. I gotta career and a family to take care of. I'm not tryna spend the rest of my days in a six by nine surrounded by concrete and steel, how about you?"

"I'll get on the line with Thorn."

"That's what I thought." Dupri said. "Tell'em to get suited and booted, we're on this tonight. We can't afford to let anyone else get a hold of them."

"Right, gimmie an hour and we'll be ready." Maza told him. "Where do you wanna meet?"

"My house," Dupri glanced at his watch. "Be here by ten o'clock."

"Gotcha," Maza said.

They both hung up.

An hour later

"I gotta plan that will rid us of our friend for good." Arsenegger said to Ortiz from across the table. They were sitting at the center of the basement. A lone light bulb hung from a chain from the ceiling illuminating a light over their heads. The detectives had bottles of Budweiser sitting beside them. Photographs of Black Jesus and Bullet were scattered over the table.

Ortiz blew smoke into the air and mashed his cigarette out in the ashtray. "What chu got up your sleeve?"

"I've been watching his daily routine for the past few days now." Arsenegger told him. "I know his schedule like the lumps on the back of my head. Every Tuesday night he and his brother go to Hollywood Park for the horse races. I figure we can sneak inside the parking lot and stick one of these puppies underneath his car." He sat a small block of an explosive on the table and Ortiz picked it up.

"This is an explosive, right?" Ortiz asked, testing the weight of the explosive.

"Yeah," Arsenegger nodded. "Makes quite the bang too, all I gotta do is press this button." He pointed to the button on the detonator in his palm.

"Ka-boom; blow that mothafucka right up." Ortiz slapped hands with Arsenegger and snapped his fingers.

Hearing the doorbell chime from upstairs, Arsenegger gathered everything up and stuffed it inside of a gymbag labeled L.A.P.D with a police shield emblazoned on it. Together, he and Ortiz headed up the staircase and into the living room.

"I'm gonna grab a cold one for the road." Arsenegger tapped Ortiz before heading into the kitchen.

"Go ahead, man. Help yourself." Ortiz told him as he headed for the front door.

As Arsenegger rummaged through the refrigerator he could hear Ortiz in the living room. "Yo, Ryan, guess who's here!" he yelled out from the living room. After Arsenegger grabbed a beer from the refrigerator, he looked through the kitchen drawer for a bottle-opener.

"You mothafuckaz are all over the news, man." Dupri told Ortiz.

"For what?" Ortiz asked curiously.

"You stood by while Ryan gunned down a young Mexican couple." Thorn filled him in. "The shit is all over the news; the police are probably on their way here now to pick you guys up."

"We gotta sneak you and Ryan outta the country before it's too late." Maza added. "Is your family here?"

"No. They're at my wife's sister's house."

"Alright, where's Ryan? We gotta get you two outta here." Dupri said.

Arsenegger stood inside of the kitchen listening to everything that was said as he took swigs of his beer. His heart quickened when he heard that there was footage on the news of him gunning down the young Mexican couple. He knew that there was no way in hell that he was going to prison for double murder. He wasn't built for prison life and he was willing to hold court in the streets if it came down to it.

"He's in the kitchen, follow…" Ortiz was cut short by the silenced whisper of a gun. The next thing Arsenegger heard was a loud thud when his body hit the floor.

Arsenegger moved to see what was going on, but before he could reach the kitchen doorway Dupri, Maza and Thorn were already coming through it. They pointed their silenced handguns at Arsenegger and he threw open the freezer and refrigerator doors. The metal subzero temperature refrigerator took the bullets meant for Arsenegger, subcoming to dents with every slug that it took. Arsenegger stooped down before the refrigerator door and held it tightly as he peered through the opening between it and the freezer door. Through it he could see all three of his former comrades blasting away at him. He stuck his burner between the openings and cracked off a few rounds, hitting Thorn in the thigh and Maza in the leg. The two men went down howling in pain. Two rounds struck Dupri's chest, but they only caused him to stagger back since he was wearing armor under his garments. Dupri took a quick moment to check on his comrades. Seeing that they only had flesh wounds, he extended his handgun before him and approached the refrigerator cautiously. Arsenegger shot out from behind the refrigerator door running toward the back porch. He threw all of his body weight into the backdoor and it broke free of its hinges, crashing to the ground. Arsenegger tucked and rolled onto the lawn of the backyard. He came up running toward the swimming pool with bullets whizzing over his head. He dived into the pool and came up on the other side, shaking the water from his head like a wet dog.

Dupri slowly approached Arsenegger with one eye closed and his gun extended before him. He had a marksman's aim and was a dead shot with any firearm. Seeing that Dupri had the drop on him, Arsenegger decided to throw in the towel.

"Alright, I give up!" he surrendered. "But tell me something before you kill me, exactly what is this all about?"

"You're a liability, Ryan. Eventually the police will bring you in and I don't have any assurance that you won't throw the dogs a bone. You were always way too reckless. We told you to calm down with all of that wild cowboy shit. Now look where it's landed you."

Arsenegger lifted his arms above the water. Dupri narrowed his eyes into slits trying to make out what was clutched in his right-palm.

"Here comes the boom." Arsenegger smiled evilly and pressed the button on the detonator. The house exploded and the fire blew Dupri forward, incinerating his limbs and leaving a torso behind. Arsenegger ducked under the water to avoid the fire ball headed in his direction. Dupri's torso splashed down into the water. As it sunk towards the bottom, Arsenegger saw the last expression he was wearing. It was one of horror. Dupri's eyes were rolled to their corners and his mouth was wide open.

Arsenegger climbed out of the swimming pool and ran toward the backyard gate, making his exit from the scene.

Meanwhile

"Ahhh," Creeper roared and punched the antique gold frame mirror in Black Jesus' living room causing it to crack into a spider's web. Black Jesus and Bullet had their heads hung in silence. They all had just seen the broadcast of Puppet and Mira being gunned down like a couple of rabid dogs in the street by Arsenegger. The breaking news report had confirmed Creeper's suspicions and he was angered that he hadn't taken Arsenegger out when he had the chance. Creeper continued to punch away at the cracked mirror in a rage, slicing up his fists and staining the glass with his own blood. All of a sudden, he stopped and turned around to Black Jesus, breathing heavily.

"I'm sorry, Jesus. I'll pay you for the mirror." Creeper told him. His eyes were bloodshot and his face was wet with tears. His cut up knuckles exposed the white meat and dripped blood onto the plush mink carpet. Creeper looked down at the mess he was making at his feet. "I'll pay for your carpet, too."

"Don't worry about it; I couldn't imagine how you may be feeling right now." Black Jesus told him sorrowfully. For the first time he noticed Creeper's sliced up hands. "Look at your hands." He took the time to examine them both; his face frowned seeing how bad they were. "Jesus Christ, Ruben, we've gotta get chu to the hospital."

"No!" Creeper snatched his bleeding hands from Black Jesus' grasp. "No hospitals. Not until I kill that piece of shit."

"Let's go find this pandejo." Bullet said with anger in his voice. He considered.

Puppet his little brother, too. And he was ready to let his gun off in his name.

"Creeper, you don't have to get your hands dirty. I have trained assassins at my disposal; they'll eat that pinche pig alive." Black Jesus assured him.

"I appreciate that, but I have to be the one to avenge Puppet's death." He told him. "He was my brother."

"I understand. If it was my blood I'd want to do the same." Black Jesus understood where he was coming from. "Before you do allow Marisol to clean your wounds and bandage your hands until you're able to go to the hospital." Creeper nodded in agreement. Black Jesus called for Marisol through the intercom in the living room. "Marisol, retrieve the first aide kit and come out into the living room, please."

Once Creeper's hands were bandaged up, he was going to set out on his mission.

Chapter Fourteen

Pavielle played the backseat of the Hummer draped in all black from head to toe. His gloved hand had a firm grip on a sawed-off double barrel shotgun as he took a bottle of Hennessy to the head. He wasn't getting liquored up for the mission at hand; it was more so for him to be able to cope with all of the turmoil he had to deal with in his hectic life. The only things that kept him going were his family and his unborn son, if it wasn't for them he'd have rather died in his coma and finally be able to be at peace.

Pavielle passed the bottle of Hennessy up front to Gouch who was also draped in all black. He wore a beanie cap and a black T-shirt. An AK-47 sat up between his legs on the floor. He guzzled some of the dark liquor from the Hennessy bottle and attempted to pass it to Gangsta.

"I'm straight." Gangsta said not bothering to look Gouch's way. His eyes were focused out of the window at the streets. He hoped that they could find Domino or Paybacc, but knew that he was probably reaching. The two of them were most likely lying low somewhere after the assault that was led against them the other night. Gangsta took tokes from a smoldering cigarette causing the tip of it to glow. He blew out smoke from his nose and allowed some to billow out of his mouth. He too was draped in all black for the mission. His thumb caressed the chamber of the black, long barreled revolver that lay on his thigh.

Draped in murder gear and riding around with the guns caused déjà vu to invade his mind. Nearly one year ago he and his protégé, Lil' Gangsta, were in this same scenario. They had followed their target to the Barbarie Coast. A dopeman by the name of Pussy had copped a half of a bird from Gangsta on consignment, but when it came time to pay he told him to "Suck my dick". Gangsta decided that it was time to give homeboy his wings. They waited until he came out of the establishment, and ended up lying him down along with the two bitches that were with him. Lil' Gangsta had gotten knocked when he was sent to discard the murder weapons and burn up the G-ride. The cheese eating mothafucka dropped a dime on Gangsta in return for his freedom. But later he ended up getting murdered by a hit-man infamously known as The Ghost.

"Fuck these niggaz at?" Gangsta asked no one in particular as he scanned the residential street.

"Them fools are probably somewhere plotting on our downfall." Gouch told Gangsta. "We aren't going to find them out here, Blood. At least not tonight we aren't."

"Look," Gangsta nodded to the windshield at a light-skinned cat on a miniature motorbike. He was in a white T-shirt and rocked a blue Texas "T" snapback upon the blue bandana that covered his head.

Gouch grinned seeing that there was someone out that night that they could blast on. The cat wasn't Domino or Paybacc, but he was from their hood and at the most his death would bring them a sense of accomplishment. "Aye, unc, he don't even see us coming. Ease up on the lil' high yellow bitch, I'ma blow his face off." He cocked the hammer on his AK-47 and took the assault rifle in both hands.

"Nah, Gucci, this one is mine." Pavielle said, sliding over to the backseat window behind the driver's seat. He gripped the sawed-off by the handle and by its barrel.

"Alright then, baby bro," Gouch said. "He's all yours."

Gangsta executed the headlights of the Hummer and creeped upon snapback. Pavielle rolled down the backseat window and stuck his sawed-off out of the window. He closed an eye and took aim with the double barrel weapon, telling Gangsta, "Easy, unc…easy." The hummer was nearly on the side of snapback once Pavielle had his sawed-off lined up with his melon. A sharp whistle got him snapback's attention. Snapback turned around with a mad dog stare, boasting the tattoos on his face. He was about to say something slick, but the sight of the sawed-off changed his mind. Snapback's face lit up in terror. His eyes bugged and his jaw dropped wide open. Then came the sound of the twin barrels as they exploded in unison. Sparks and smoke spilled from the mouth of the barrels, ripping snapback's face clean off. The only thing left behind was his bloody, skeletal bone structure. Gangsta mashed the accelerator burning rubber down the block and leaving black tire prints in his wake. Pavielle looked out the back window of the Hummer. He watched as snapback rode a little ways on his mini motorbike before crashing into the back of a parked Scion and falling out into the street.

It was just another day in the hood.

$$$

The night was as silent as the grave, and so dark that you could barely make out the silhouettes outside of Pavielle's home. The Muslims necks were on swivels, it being the only thing on them moving, made their bodies seem like hardened clay moldings. They operated and moved like robots and were only there to carry out orders: protect Vayda at all costs. That was their priority, and each man would lay his life down if need be.

The sound of a sawed-off shotgun echoing far in the distance didn't move the Muslims. They were used to the sounds of gunfire going off in the middle of the night. They were in the heart of the ghetto. They were in an area known as The Low Bottoms. A section of the lower Eastside that had a reputation for getting it popping, it was known for violence and gang activity. And during the few months that the Muslims were posted there guarding their charge they had grown accustomed to it.

A lone man rocking a black leather duster moved fluidly up the block. Stopping, he slid a cigarette in between his lips and fished around in his pocket for a lighter. When he couldn't find one he patted down his person, but still came up empty handed. Seeing the Muslims posted up in the yard of a house, he decided to make his way inside and see if they had a light. As soon as the man entered the yard the Muslims assembled around a fellow Muslim wearing a red bowtie. When Nasheed wasn't present, red bowtie was the brother in charge.

"Can we help you, brotha?" red bowtie asked.

"Yes, brotha, you wouldn't happen to have a light, would ya?" the man inquired.

"I'm sorry, but I don't smoke."

The man nodded his head. He spat the cigarette on the ground and mashed it out under his boot heel. One by one, the Muslims hollered in excruciation as respective bullets struck their forms, causing them to collapse in a domino effect. Red bowtie whipped out his cannon and slowly backed away, his head whipping from left to right trying to see what angle the sniper was launching his attack from. When he saw the man in the duster moving towards the house he pointed his cannon at his chest, freezing him in his tracks.

"Get your hands up! Get your hands up now!" red bowtie barked, forgetting about the sniper that had just had him on high alert a moment ago. His only priority was to protect Vayda from any threat coming her way. The man in the duster slowly raised his hands in surrender and rolled his eyes, he was annoyed with red bowtie.

"You do know you're in a situation that you can't win, right?" Paybacc asked.

"Shut up! Shut your…" red bowtie's left-eye burst, leaving a bloody and gaping hole behind that you could see clean through. His limp body hit the ground on its back and he released his gun. Paybacc turned around and gave a signal to someone in the night that wasn't visible. He grabbed red bowtie's body under its arms and dragged it up the steps of the front porch.

$$$

Vayda was sitting on the couch with Damu's head resting in her lap. She caressed his head and talked with Nasheed who was trying to fix the flat-screen with the fuzzy picture.

"So how long have you been a member of the nation?" she asked.

"Ten years now, Ms. Vayda." He said down on his knees with his shirt's sleeve rolled up as he toyed with the flat-screen.

"Are you married? Got any kids?" Vayda asked, then paused and said, "I'm sorry I'm all up in yours."

"It's quite alright, Ms. Vayda." Nasheed said. "I am not married, and no I don't have any children. Ah, there we go." He smiled, having just fixed the flat-screen.

"Yay," Vayda smiled and clapped her hands excitedly. "Now we can watch the Sex in the city movie, Damu." She looked down at the rotweiler and ruffled his head. "Thanks, Nasheed. I really appreciate it."

"No problem, Ms. Vayda." Nasheed replied, pulling down the sleeves of his button-down and buttoning the cuffs. There was a knock at the door that stole his attention. He approached the door and said, "Who is it?"

"It's me, brotha!" a voice replied that Nasheed couldn't distinguish through the door. Figuring that it was one of his fellow Muslim brothers, Nasheed open the wood door first. Once he saw that it was red bowtie he went ahead and opened the iron door. As soon as he undone the lock, red bowtie's corpse was thrown on him. Nasheed fell to the floor under the weight of the dead body. He looked to the kitchen and saw his shoulder holsters with his gun in it hanging onto the back of a chair. He'd hung it there when Vayda called him inside to fix the flat-screen for her.

Paybacc stepped inside over Nasheed and the dead body, setting his sights on Vayda. Vayda was terrified. She got to her feet and ran down the hallway toward her bedroom. Damu stood up in the couch barking ferociously at the intruder. Paybacc attempted to go after Vayda but the beast rushed him. Paybacc lifted his forearm and Damu bit down into it. The Rottweiler jerked from left to right violently, trying to tear a chunk out of the intruder's arm.

$$$

Vayda ran into her bedroom and slammed the door closed behind her, locking it. She got beside the nightstand and pushed it against the bedroom door. She grabbed the telephone off of the nightstand and punched in Pavielle's number. Vayda was going to call the police but she knew if they rushed the spot that they'd snoop around the house and would eventually find the guns and blocks of cocaine Pavielle had stashed there. She'd just gotten her fiancé back from the cold grips of Death and she didn't want to end up losing him to the system. So she decided to hold down the fort until her man was able to make it home. Pavielle had taken her to the shooting range numerous times, and she hoped that she'd trained well enough to protect herself and their baby.

Vayda held the phone to her ear as she opened the closet. She parted the clothes and exposed a shotgun hiding at the back of it. She took a tin box off the top shelf in the closet and walked it over to the bed. She sat down on the bed, opened the tin box, and removed a box of shells. Next, she dumped the contents of the box out onto the bed and began loading the shells into the shotgun, one by one.

"Pavy, you gotta hurry home!" she said in a panic. "This big guy has broken into the house, I think it's Paybacc! I barricaded myself in our bedroom and I got the…hello? Hello?" she said into the phone hearing the line go dead. Then the lights went out. She tossed the phone aside and took cover beside the bed with her shotgun trained on the door.

$$$

"Floor this mothafucka, Paybacc is hitting my house, Blood!" Pavielle yelled to Gangsta from the backseat once the line had went dead on Vayda. He began reloading shells into his sawed-off. Gouch brought his AK-47 from off of the floor and into his lap, gripping it tightly. As soon as they pulled up at the house he was hopping out and laying everyone down he wasn't familiar with.

"Shit!" Gangsta mashed his cigarette out in the ashtray and put on his seatbelt. He adjusted the rearview mirror and mashed the accelerator, gunning through redlights and stop signs.

$$$

Damu still had a lock on Paybacc's arm and was whipping his head from side to side wildly. Paybacc grimaced and bit the dog on top of the head, but it didn't faze him. So he whipped out his banger and cracked him over the skull with it as hard as he could. When the Rottweiler still wouldn't release him, he pressed his steel to the side of its neck and pulled the trigger. Damu yelped and hit the floor dead, tongue hanging out the side of its mouth.

Paybacc took a moment to admire his handiwork. He turned to red bowtie's corpse ready to finish off Nasheed and found that he was gone. He whipped around to the kitchen and Nasheed had just pulled his burner from his holster, which was hanging on the back of the chair. Nasheed whipped around with his gun at the same time Paybacc was lifting his banger. They pulled the triggers of their weapons in succession, each taking bullets from one anothers guns. Paybacc recoiled with each shot that he took and so did Nasheed. The two opposing factors wore expressions of pain as they carried on until Nasheed's gun clicked empty. Even after his banger's magazine was spent, Nasheed continued to pull the trigger of his gun. Finally realizing there wasn't a shell left; he tossed his weapon aside and slid down to the floor, leaning against the chair of the kitchen table. Nasheed glared up at Paybacc as he bled out, his white button-down was covered with blood stains. It almost looked as if he was wearing a red button-down shirt.

Paybacc stood erect staring Nasheed in the eyes with a smug grin. He knocked on his chest; it was covered by bodyarmor. The lights went out, but Paybacc didn't even flinch as he approached his victim, who hadn't taken his glare from off of him. Paybacc lifted his banger to the Nasheed's forehead. The Muslim kept his glare on his would be killer as he spat on the floor. He wasn't afraid to die. The Nation had prepared him for worse things.

"Assalama Alaikum." Paybacc said to Nasheed, which meant "Peace be unto you" before sending him off to meet Allah. Nasheed was slumped where he sat, the gaping hole in his forehead dripped blood onto the crotch of his slacks.

Domino came running through the door with a banger in his waistline and a sniper rifle in his hands, ready to let something fly. Paybacc spun around with his gun arm erect and they nearly shot each other. Identifying who one another was they lowered their weapons.

"I killed the lights, but I'm not sure if I got the phone-line in time." Domino reported. "For all we know The Ones are on their way, maybe even Booby and the rest of them niggaz."

"Fuck the police and fuck Booby. His time is coming." Paybacc ejected the empty magazine from his banger and smacked in a fresh one, chambering a round in the head.

"Go around back to the bedroom and bust out the window, keep your gun on her. But be careful, cuz, she probably strapped by now. The bitch is a hustler's wife. If Booby was smart he taught her how to use a tool. I'll going through the door." Domino gave him a nod before running out of the house to carry out his orders. As soon as he had made his departure Paybacc moved towards the master bedroom's door.

$$$

Vayda sat on the floor with her shotgun trained on the door of the bedroom. She was locked, loaded, and ready to kill if need be. Suddenly, the doorknob sounded as it twisted and turned from someone on the other side trying to gain entree. Vayda braced the stock of her shotgun against her shoulder and let it roar twice, blowing chunks out of the door. The bedroom window was shattered by the butt of a sniper rifle, which startled her.

"Leave me the fuck alone!" Vayda screamed with tears rolling down her face. She swung her shotgun around and pulled the trigger, blowing out what was left of the broken glass. She swung back around to the bedroom door, hearing it rattle as some one kicked on it. The door broke loose from its hinges and with each kick after, the nightstand was being forced back into the bedroom. Vayda let her shotgun bark twice more, hoping to kill or seriously injure whoever was on the other side of the door. Unbeknownst to her, the barrel of a sniper rifle slid in at the corner of the broken bedroom window.

"Bitch, drop the gun!" Domino barked. "Drop the gun now!"

"Fuck you!" Vayda barked back, and gave her shotgun the freedom to reply once again. Still holding onto the sniper rifle, Domino leaned against the house avoiding the buck shots of the 12 gauge.

Bloom! Bloom!

The bedroom door rattled again as it was being kicked by a force to be reckoned with. Vayda braced the shotgun against her shoulder and waited for the intruder to come inside, so she could blow his fucking head off. Hearing the crunching of glass at her rear, she swung the shotgun back around to it.

"Drop the fucking shotgun, before I shoot your stupid ass!" Domino yelled angrily. His face was twisted into a mask of aggravation.

Vayda wiped the tears from her face with the back of her hand and sniffled, gripping the shotgun tighter. If she was going to die then she was going to die defending her life and the one growing inside of her.

"Not a fucking chance, nigga!" she blasted on the window once again.

Bloom!

Vayda swung back around with her shotgun ready to stop someone's heart beat. The bedroom door was almost all of the way open now. She couldn't see Paybacc, but she could see his shadow on the hallway wall.

"Redbone, I suggest you give it up. You got about one more round left in that shotty. If you force us to drag this out any longer, when I finally do get my hands on you, we're going to play doctor. I'm gonna carve that baby outta your belly, then I'm gonna use its umbilical cord to choke you to death with it. You feel me? Don't be stupid!" his eyebrows arched and his nose scrunched up.

Vayda sobbed uncontrollably with green snot threatening to drip out of her nose. She was stuck between a rock and a hard place. She was confused and didn't know what to do. Both she and her baby's lives were in jeopardy. The decisions she had to make could forever alter their lives, or make it so that they wouldn't have one. Vayda didn't know Paybacc, but from what Gangsta had told her he was one despicable human being. Some of the stories she heard about him could have a person waking up in the middle of the night in cold sweats. One in particular was a recent one where he'd chopped off some kid's feet and threw them over a powerline like they were a couple of old sneakers. She thought that if he could do that to a kid then he wasn't past butchering a pregnant woman, especially one that was his enemy's fiancé.

Vayda figured that it would be better for her to surrender and take her chances as a hostage. She would willingly go with Paybacc and Domino in hopes of finding a way to escape their clutches later. At least that way she and her baby would have a fighting chance. With one shell left and two guns on her there was no way that she could fight Domino and Paybacc off for much longer. With the threat of losing her baby hovering over her crown of curly hair, Vayda decided to throw in the towel.

"All right, I give up!" Vayda threw down the shotgun and slowly got to her feet, raising her hands into the air. Paybacc stepped into the bedroom with his banger trained on her, instructing her to get down on her knees with her back to him. She did as he said, and he tucked his banger on his waistline. Paybacc produced a roll of silver duct-tape. He taped up Vayda's mouth and bounded her wrists. He then pulled a black pillow case from within his duster and pulled it down over her head.

A few minutes later

Gangsta, Gouch and Pavielle ran up the steps and entered the house like a hit squad, waving their weapons around. Pavielle called out Vayda's name as he went from room to room in search of her. He never received a reply. He tactifully entered their bedroom and found the window wide open; a cool breeze blew in and disturbed the curtains. Pavielle ran over to the window and stuck his head out of it. Looking from left to right, he saw that there was no one in sight, so he pulled his head back in and shut the window. He headed back into the living room where he'd left Gangsta and Gouch.

"They took her, she's gone." Pavielle reported to his brother and uncle, regretfully.

"Was there anything left behind? Like a note or something?" Gangsta asked.

"No. Nothing like…" the words died in Pavielle throat once he saw Damu strewn out dead; his tongue hanging out of the side of his mouth. He pulled the stocking cap from off of his head as he approached Damu. He sat down on the floor and laid his sawed-off beside him. Pavielle pulled his dog over into his lap. His eyes became glassy as he gently stroked the beast's shiny black coat. Damu had been like family to him. The blood that coursed through him may as well have been the blood that coursed through Pavielle, Gouch and Gangsta. Pavielle kissed Damu on top of the head and tears trickled down, raining droplets on the Rottweiler. Gangsta and Gouch stood by with their heads hung; they knew how Pavielle felt about the dog.

Gangsta looked to the kitchen and saw Nasheed sitting on the floor slumped, marinating in his own blood as red droplets fell from the gaping hole in his forehead. Gangsta shook his head and crossed his heart in the sign of he crucifix.

Chapter Fifteen

Beth, Detective Arsenegger's wife, sat up in bed under the covers with the telephone cradled to her ear. A late night infomercial played on the flat-screen, but the TV was on mute, so she could hear everything that was being said to her over the telephone.

"We're fine, everything is OK." Beth said into the telephone. "What about you?"

"I'm all right." Arsenegger told her. "Has anybody come over there to ask you any questions?"

"A few reporters and journalists, and some detectives."

"What did the detectives ask?"

"A bunch of questions about you, but I denied knowing anything."

"Well, listen, I got to go, this call could be being traced. I give you a call sometime tomorrow."

"OK. I love you." Her voice cracked with emotion and she wiped the tears that ran down her pale white cheeks.

"I love you, too. Tell my little princess the same and give her a kiss for me."

They both hung up.

Beth threw he covers off of her person and hopped out of bed. She journeyed out of her bedroom and down the hallway, still wiping the tears from her eyes. Nearing her daughter's bedroom, she saw a small light illuminating from it out into the hallway wall. Then there was a gentle voice humming a lullaby. Hearing this caused her forehead to indent and she sped walked toward's her daughter's bedroom. She turned the corner into the doorway and her heart dropped. A young Mexican man in a trench coat was sitting on the side of Tonai as she slept, gently sweeping the strands of hair from out of her face. A jovial expression was on his face as he continued to hum the tune as if she wasn't even there.

"Who the fuck are you? What're you doing in my house?" Beth asked with her hand over heart, she thought she was about to have a heart attack.

"Shhh," Creeper hushed her with his gun to his lips. "You'll wake her up. She's beautiful. She reminds me of my kid sister, Arlene." He looked back to Tonai and smiled.

"What do you want from us?" Beth's voice cracked with emotion and a new set of tears spilled down her face.

Creeper pulled the covers over Tonai and rose to his feet. He stood facing Beth with his Colt .45 held at his side. "All I want to know is the whereabouts of your husband and we'll be on our marry way."

Beth narrowed her eyes into slits and tilted her head to the side. "*We'll* be on our marry *way*?"

"Yes, *we*," Creeper repeated.

"Oh, my God," her eyes bugged and she ran out of Tonai's bedroom, nearly falling. For all she knew the house was crawling with Creeper's minions. She had to get to the .380 that her husband kept at the back of the closet in a shoebox if she was going to have a chance. She turned the corner through the doorway of her bedroom and ran dead smack into Bullet. He looked down at her with his hazel green eyes and smiled fiendishly, licking his top lip. Beth ran from out of the bedroom and he tripped her up, causing her to hit the floor. Bullet whipped out his Glock .40. He grabbed a lock of Beth's hair and pulled her to her feet violently, nearly yanking strands of hair from her scalp. She hollered out in pain and he forced her back into Tonai's bedroom, telling her to shut the fuck up.

"White bread, if I have to tell you one more time about your mouth, I'm going to let my friend there give you a reason to holler, you hear?" Creeper said with a stern look. His eyebrows were arched and his lips were peeled back in a sneer.

"Oh, Vanilla," Bullet said excitedly licking the side of Beth's face with his long tongue, leaving a wet streak behind.

Beth closed her eyes and calmed herself down. She nodded and said, "I got it."

"Good. Now, tell us where your husband is." Creeper said to her.

"I...I don't know."

"What's your name?"

"Be...Beth."

"Beth, you don't expect me to believe that, do you?"

"I'm telling you the truth."

Creeper nodded and pointed his Colt .45 at Tonai's head. "If you don't tell me where your husband is, I'm going to splatter your little girl's skull all over this headboard. Now, I don't wanna do it but you're forcing my hand. So you make the choice, either your husband or your daughter. It's all on you."

"Fuck you!" Beth spat his way.

"Fuck me? Nah, puto, fuck you," Creeper picked up a stuffed animal from beside Tonai. He placed it over her head and pressed his .45 into it to muffle the bark of his gun. He stared Beth dead in her eyes as he slowly began to apply pressure to the trigger. Creeper wore a hard face; if Beth was trying to call his bluff she was going to regret it. Seeing the trigger gradually being pulled back, she panicked.

"OK, ok, ok!" she hollered, causing Tonai to stir in her sleep.

Creeper took the stuffed animal from the little girl's head and tucked his .45 on his waistline.

"Where is he?" he asked terrified Beth.

"The address is in my bedroom."

"OK. My friend will take you to get it." Creeper sat back down beside Tonai watching her sleep.

$$$

Arsenegger was laying low in a four bedroom house out in Glendale. It was one of three homes that he owned thanks to the blood money he and Ortiz had gotten jacking D-boys and making big time hustlers pay taxes. Over time he'd vasted a small fortune and was able to live far more comfortably than he would have been on a homicide detectives salary. The house was under a deceased friend's name so he didn't have to worry about the police kicking down the door looking for him. He was free to sit back, relax, and kick his feet up for a time.

Running away was was the farthest thing from Arsenegger's mind; he was going to do just the opposite. He was still going to set the bomb under Black Jesus' car at the Hollywood race track. There was no way he wasn't going to carry out that hit. He reasoned that his life was already going down the shitter, so what did he have to lose with going ahead with the mission? He wasn't done with Gangsta and his clan either; he had a cake baking for them. He was just waiting for the perfect time to set it off on them. Once he was done exacting his revenge on his enemies, he was going to get his family and disappear to an island somewhere far off of the coast. They'd assume different aliases, dye their hair, and get plastic surgery so they'd go under the radar. Their friends and family would think that they'd just vanished off of the face of the earth, and that's exactly how he wanted it. To him it was the only way he could see being able to live the rest of his life in peace.

Arsenegger sat at the dining room table with his head bowed and his hands clasped saying grace over his meal. The plate before him consisted of a whole lobster, a medium rare T-bone steak and mashed potatos. To drink he had a glass of grape wine, and for dessert he planned on having a slice of cheese cake.

Wrapping up his prayer, Arsenegger stuffed a cloth inside of his collar. He picked up a fork and a knife and dug into his meal. Once he finished his cheese cake, he plopped down on the couch and cracked open a bottle of beer. He propped his feet upon the coffee-table and watched CSI until began to nod off. Arsenegger turned off the TV and headed up stairs. He took of his Hawaiian shirt and hung it on the back of the door. He was just about to remove his shoulder holster when something crashed through his bedroom window, shattering the glass. He looked to the floor and a brick was there with a note rubber-banded around it. He picked up the brick, removed the note and unfolded it. It read: *Bring your punk ass outside!*

Arsenegger crept to the broken window and took a peek outside. In the backyard there was a Mexican dude in a trench coat staring up at him. A light bulb came on inside of Arsenegger's head. He remembered the young man's face from the sushi restaurant in West Hollywood. He was with Black Jesus and Gangsta. Having remembered this, he knew he had trouble on his hands so he whipped out his banger from his holster and stormed down the steps. He pulled open the glass sliding doors that lead out into the backyard and stepped out. Creeper stood before him empty handed, glaring at him.

"You know that young Mexican kid and that girl you shot down? Well, that kid was my younger brother." Creeper glared up at him with trembling lips, looking like a hostile stray dog. This was the Mexican man that he saw from his window that was dressed in a trench coat.

"You're about to join'em!" Arsenegger went to point his banger at Creeper, but the sound of a shotgun being racked caused him to freeze. His eyes darted to their corners; Bullet was there with a shotgun trained on his temple ready to blow his skull apart.

"Not tonight, homes. You and my homeboy gotta get down." Bullet told him with one eye closed as he braced the stock of the shotgun against his shoulder.

"That's right, I'ma kick your ass, then I'm gonna send you to make peace with your Lord and Savior." Creeper removed his trench coat and tossed it aside. He kissed the gold Virgin Mary medallion of Puppet's that hung from his neck and tucked it inside of his shirt. He stretched his limbs and bent his back, preparing to brawl with the snake ass detective.

Arsenegger tucked his banger back into its holster and tossed it aside. He then pulled off his undershirt leaving himself bear chested. He cracked his knuckles and slid into a fighting stance. "I'm gonna beat you into the fucking ground, boy." He spat to the ground.

"We'll see, pig." Creeper said behind a hard face, in a fighting stance with his fists in front of him.

Creeper and Arsenegger engaged each other like a couple of heavy weight fighters, sizing one another up. Arsenegger threw a couple jabs, but he easily dodged them. He waited for Arsenegger to attempt to jab him again and unleashed a three punch combination on the center of his face causing his eyes to water and his face to turn red.

"Unh huh, I hit hard don't I, bitch?" Creeper said to him, seeing the pain in his face. Angry, Arsenegger went in for a combination of his own and ended with an upper cut that hit nothing but air. Creeper hit him with a gut punch that knocked the wind out of him and made him clutch his stomach.

"That's right, Creeper, fuck'em up, homie!" Bullet egged his homeboy on with the shotgun resting over his shoulder.

Creeper rained blows on Arsenegger's exposed face, breaking his nose and making his eyes bloodshot. He landed a hard right into his chin that made him hobble on one leg before eventually falling to the ground.

"Ooof!" he lay their wincing in pain.

"It's exactly what I thought; you aren't shit without a pistola." Creeper watched as Arsenegger slowly attempted to get up from the ground.

The sound of spinning perpellers filled the air causing Creeper and Bullet look up into the sky. There was a police helicopter headed their way.

"Go ahead, finish this, punk!" Bullet urged his homie, having seen Arsenegger was back on his feet. His face looked like it had been beaten with some sort of blunt object, but it had only been pounded by Creeper's fists. Creeper wasn't that big of a man, but his punches were equivalent to those of a muscle bound three-hundred pound man. Arsenegger looked to be in pretty bad shape. He was standing on wobbily legs and his face was swollen.

"Come on, tortilla dip!" Arsenegger taunted through busted lips.

"You got balls, I'll give you that." Creeper teetered back and forth from foot to foot, bobbing and weaving Arsenegger's punches. He closed in, slamming his fists into each side of his ribs, breaking them. He closed the deal with an upper cut that threw his ass off his feet and onto his back. Arsenegger lazily looked around as if he didn't know where he was.

"Piece of shit," Creeper spat on his face as he stood over him. The goo slithered over Arsenegger's swollen shut eye. Bullet threw Creeper his trench coat and he slipped it on. Turning around he saw Arsenegger pull a .38 special from his ankle holster. He was about to point it at Creeper, but he managed to kick the piece from his hand. "Dirty mothafucka," Creeper spat heatedly. He whipped his Colt .45 from around his back and was about to blow a hole through Arsenegger's forehead when he heard a loud crash. He looked to the sliding glass doors and saw the police pouring inside armed to the teeth. Creeper tucked his burner into his back and signaled for Bullet to follow him. Together, they hopped the fence into the neighboring yard and fled the scene.

The police helicopter shined its bright light upon Arsenegger as he lie on the ground groaning in pain. The police stepped outside surrounding him. One of them snapped the handcuffs around his wrists while another read him his rights.

Beth had called the police and gave them her husband's whereabouts. She'd rather see him alive behind glass then in the ground below a tombstone.

Chapter Sixteen

Vayda's wrists were handcuffed above her head around a pipe in the ceiling. Her head was hung and she was standing on her toes to keep from hanging. The house was in ruin and not inhabitable. There were tears in the hardwood floors and large holes in every wall. A rodent scampered across the floor so fast that it was nothing more than a blur in motion. It had almost made it into the gaping hole in the wall until a size ten, navy blue Cortez stomped on it. The attack killed it instantly and caused it to ooze with blood. The Cortez kicked the rodent across the room. It smacked into the wall and hit the floor.

"All of these mothafucking rats around here, cuz. Goddamn!" Domino scowled and twisted his lips. He continued walking around the room sharpening his bowie knife on a sharpening block. The metal clashing with the block made a reoccurring *clinging* sound. Once he was done, he sat the block on the mantle of what used to be a fireplace. He poked his index finger with the tip of the knife and drew a dot of blood. He sucked the blood from his finger and looked to

Vayda. He walked over to her and grabbed a lock of her hair. He pulled her head back and stared into her eyes. Although her face was slick with tears, her eyes were burning with rage. She gritted her teeth as she locked into a stare with Domino. He traced her face with the knife and allowed the blade to travel over her breasts and onto her round belly.

"The boy Booby has taste, you're a bad bitch; pregnant and all." Domino complimented as his eyes took her in from head to toe, with a sadistic smile stretching his lips. Suddenly, Vayda lunged forth and bit his nose causing him to scream out in pain. He staggered back and touched his nose, coming away with bloody finger tips. He looked up at Vayda and snarled. He hauled off and punched her in the chin, knocking her out cold. The blow left her head hanging and her knees bent as she snored asleep."Red ass bitch," He used his shirt to wipe his bleeding nose.

Paybacc laughed. "That's what cho ass get, nigga, all in that broad's face." He said from the kitchen counter where he sat loading slugs into his Tec-9. Once he finished loading up his tool, he sat it aside and picked up Vayda's cell phone.

"Be quiet, cuz, I'ma 'bout to call these fools." He told Domino as he scrolled through the cell looking for Booby's number. He figured he was the one stored under "Hubby" so he pressed *call* and held the phone to his ear.

$$$

Pavielle, Gouch and Killa Dre sat around the dining room while Gangsta paced the floor back and forth with his hands behind his back. Locked and loaded automatic weapons lay scattered on the table. They all impatiently waited for a very important phone call. Suddenly, a cell phone rang at the center of the dining room table. Its screen lit up and it danced around on the red oak wood table. Everyone froze in place and exchanged glances. Pavielle placed a finger to his lips, signaling them to be quiet while he answered the call. He picked up the cellular and pressed *talk*. He placed the cell to his ear and said "hello" into it. He listened intently as he scribbled down what he was being told on a Los Angeles Times news paper. Once he was done, he dropped the ink pen and sat back in his chair. He listened to the last of what the caller was telling him before pressing *end* and sitting the cell phone down on the table. He looked around and noticed that all eyes were on him in anticipation of what he had to say.

"He wants me at this address." Pavielle told Gangsta and Gouch, pointing to the address on the news paper he'd written down. "He wants me to come alone. I'll give him me in exchange for Vayda."

"That's it? That's the deal?" Gangsta asked. Pavielle nodded.

"Going wherever this fool wants you to go is like suicide. There is no doubt in my mind that he's going to kill you." Gouch stated as he massaged his chin. "Nah, we've gotta come up with a plan to get Vayda back."

"Gouch is right, Blood. We've gotta cook something up, we're not finna let chu be led into a slaughter like cattle." Killa Dre chimed in.

"It's all on me." Gangsta said, sitting on the edge of the table with his leg slightly propped upon it.

"What chu mean?" Gouch asked,frowning and sitting up in his chair.

"It's because of me that this cock sucka is alive to wreak havoc on our lives. If I would have pushed this nigga back in the day we wouldn't have this problem." Gangsta admitted what he believed was true.

"That's bullshit. If it wasn't Paybacc then it would have been Domino, or one of Nightmare's other homeboys." Pavielle told him.

"Maybe so but it's Paybacc that has claimed the throne, so this makes him my responsibility by default." Gangsta reasoned. He took a deep breath and folded his large arms across his chest. "Y'all fallback and let me handle this. I'll take care of it."

"By yourself?" Gouch shot to his feet with a frown plastered on his face. "No fucking way, unc. Unh unh. I'm not having it. I'm rolling out witchu, and these are accompanying us." He held up his twin Berettas and rubbed them against each other. The guns made their own music.

"I'm going too; y'all are all of the family that I have, besides moms. It's ride or die, with me." Killa Dre rose to his feet, picking up one of the automatic weapons from the table.

"We're all riding then." Pavielle grabbed one of the automatic weapons as he stood to his feet.

Gangsta looked over everyone and grinned. The collective were the spawns of his gangster, and that made him proud. "Alright then." He nodded and stood to his feet picking up one of the automatic weapons. He approached Pavielle still grinning. Pavielle looked at him like *What the fuck are you staring at?* Suddenly, Gangsta cracked him in the chin and knocked him out cold. Pavielle lay on the floor snoring like an obese man with a heart problem. Next, Gangsta turned to Gouch and said, "Gucci, drag him into momma's bedroom and lock the door. I can't let Booby ride with us. He's gotta be alive to raise his son." Gouch nodded. He grabbed Booby under his arms and dragged him into G-momma's bedroom. He laid him in the bed. While he was getting him situated, Gangsta cracked him across the back of the skull with his weapon, knocking him out cold. He then closed the bedroom door and locked it behind him.

"I guess it's just me and you on this mission, huh?" Killa Dre asked, gripping the automatic weapon with both hands.

"Nah, I need you to babysit." Gangsta gripped his shoulder. "Watch over my nephews and make sure they're ok. This nigga Paybacc play the game dirtier than most, so there's no telling what he has baking in the oven for'em."

"But chu are gonna need somebody out there to watch your back." Killa Dre reasoned. He desperately wanted to tag along to make sure that his big homie was ok.

"God's got my back, lil' homie, God and this four fever." Gangsta patted the bulge of his waistline where his chrome .45 automatic rested. "This is a O.G call. I don't need no talk back. Just do like I say. You claim you're a soldier, right? Well, that's what soldier's do, they follow orders. You got me?" Killa Dre nodded. "Alright," He patted his shoulder.

$$$

A gold GT Bentley pulled up alongside the curb outside a condemned house. Gangsta hopped out and grabbed a black briefcase from out of the trunk. He slammed the trunk closed and stepped upon the porch of the condemned house. He knocked on the door. He could hear someone shuffling around before the door was unlocked and pulled open. Paybacc shoved his Tec-9 into his face and peered around both corners of the doorway.

"Fuck is Booby?" he asked Gangsta, mad dogging his mothafucking ass.

"He couldn't make it, but I figured you and I can work something out."

Paybacc yanked Gangsta inside and slammed the door behind him. He shoved him against the wall and kicked his legs apart roughly with his foot. He placed the barrel of his Tec-9 to the back of his dome while he gave him a pat down that produced a chrome .45 automatic handgun. Paybacc turned Gangsta around and held the .45 automatic in his face with his index and thumb. "What's up with this?" he asked him of the gun.

"Did you think I was going to waltz in here butt ass naked? You know how Gs move, be serious now." Gangsta straighten out his suit and adjusted his tie.

Paybacc nodded in understanding and tucked Gangsta's .45 automatic at his back. He looked down at the black briefcase then back up at Gangsta. "What's in the briefcase?"

"My proposition, I'ma businesss man," Gangsta smirked. "There's one million dollars in cash inside there, notta penny less. All I want you to do is leave me and my family alone and it's all yours. You go on living your life and we'll go on living ours."

"There's one million dollars in this briefcase?" Paybacc asked with disbelief, pointing his Tec-9 down at the briefcase. Gangsta nodded. The mountain of muscle narrowed his eyes into slits as he stared at his old enemy. "Bullshit, I open that briefcase and something's going to explode in my face. You must think I'm stupid. You open that mothafucka up." He pointed the Tec-9 in the O.G's face.

"No problem." Gangsta said, kneeling down to the briefcase and popping its locks. Paybacc stepped back holding his Tec-9 to his forehead. If he tried anything funny he was going to send some hot shit through his face. Gangsta opened the briefcase and pulled out four bands, holding two in each hand. "See." He said, laying the bands on the floor. With the hand he used to hold the Tec-9 in, Paybacc motioned for him to back up against the wall. Once the O.G followed orders, Paybacc turned the briefcase around with his foot so it would be facing him. He kept his Tec-9 trained on Gangsta as he went through the bands stacked up inside the briefcase. He'd gotten half way to the bottom before stopping and stacking the bands back inside. A smile emerged on his face having seen he'd come up on an easy million bucks. He locked the briefcase and picked it up by the handle.

"Alright, you gotta deal, but I want chu to take that bounty off of my head." Paybacc told him.

"It's done." Gangsta replied, grinning harder now that he'd struck a deal.

"Get redbone and you can bounce." He motioned over to Vayda with his Tec-9. He then tossed Gangsta the key to the handcuffs that bounded Vayda.

When Gangsta saw Vayda hanging from the pipe unconscious, he frowned. "Fuck did you do to her?" he asked.

"She wouldn't behave so thehomie knocked her out cold, besides that she's straight." Paybacc assured him.

When Gangsta stood on his toes to unlock Vayda's handcuffs, he was grabbed by the front of his shirt. Vayda's mop of curly hair turned up and he met the devious eyes of Domino. Domino grunted as he plunged something into Gangsta's belly, causing his eyes to bug. Gangsta's jaw dropped and he felt a seering pain shoot through his belly. He howled in pain as Domino continued to work his bowie knife in and out of his belly, while walking him backwards. Domino yanked his bowie knife out of his victim's belly, spilling droplets of blood at his feet. Still holding Gangsta by the front of his shirt, he kissed him on the cheek. It was 'The Kiss of Death'. Gangsta fell flat on his back holding his stomach. He kicked his right-leg as he bawled in excruciation. Domino pulled off the curly wig and tossed it aside. Using the back of his hand, he wiped the lip-stick from his mouth and dropped the bowie knife. He was draped in the clothes that Vayda was wearing when he and Paybacc had abducted her.

"Life's a bitch, and then you die." Paybacc shook his head. He pulled Gangsta's .45 automatic from around his back and handed it over to Domino. "I'm finna bounce up outta here. Clap old girl and meet me back at the crib so we can divide the spoils." He said to his homeboy and held up the briefcase.

Domino took the chrome .45 into his blood stained hands. Once Paybacc had left the house, he walked through the doorway of the master bedroom and opened the closet. Vayda was in the corner of the closet. She was in her bra and panties. Her mouth was gagged and her wrists were bound. Her eyes traveled up from Domino's Nike Cortez to his cold eyes, they didn't display any remorse. He wore a solemn expression as he lifted the .45 automatic and aimed it at her skull. Suddenly, his body jerked and his eyes bugged. His lips parted and blood spilled over his chin. He looked down and a long rusted pipe was sticking out of his belly, dripping blood from its sharp end. Domino made to turn around and he was lifted off of his feet, legs dangling in the air. He hollered out as he began to slide back further on the rusty pipe, coating it with his own blood.

"Rahhhhhh," Domino threw his face back screaming bloody murder with a wincing face. Reactively, he fired off his .45 automatic into the air, but eventually dropped it.

Gangsta slung the rusted pipe aside with Domino still impaled on it. He lay on the floor bawling in agony and trying to pull the pipe out of his belly, hands becoming slippery. Gangsta watched as he kicked and squirmed around, trying to pull the pipe from out of his torso. Domino's movements began to grow slower until they stopped all together. Gangsta pulled the knife that Domino used to stab him with from his waistline and cut Vayda free from her restraints and gag. Once he was done, he sat down on the floor of the closet and laid his head back in the corner, holding his stomach as blood trickled from the corner of his mouth.

"Oh, my God, you're hurt! You're hurt bad!" Vayda's forehead creased with worry lines. She'd just moved Gangsta's hands aside and examining his wounds. "We've gotta get chu outta here." She told him and tried to help him to his feet.

"No…no…" Gangsta shook his head, wincing. "It's too late for me…it's too late."

"No, it's not." Vayda told him as tears ran down her face. She pulled his cell phone from out of his suit's jacket and called 9-1-1. She gave them the address where they were and hung up. Gangsta held up a remote control that was attached to the ring on his car keys. "What? What is this?" she asked taking the remote control.

"Press the button…press the button now!" Gangsta commanded before hanging his head. Vayda tried to wake him up, but he wouldn't come to. She pressed her ear to his left-breast and heard his heart beat. "Hold on, Gangsta. You've got to hold on, we need you." She told him as she held up his face with both hands. Gangsta eyes were barely open. He mumbled something that was inaudible to Vayda, so she listened closer.

"OK." Gangsta said weakly.

Vayda stood erect and pressed the button on the remote control. She heard a loud explosion and felt the ground quake.

Afterwards, she heard car alarms going off in the distance. She stepped out of the closet and walked out onto the front porch. Looking down the street, she saw smoke rising in the air from a far. Hearing screeching tires come to a stop, she turned around. A black Mercedes Benz was in the middle of the street. Pavielle, Gouch and Killa Dre all hopped out with their fingers settled on the triggers of their weapons. Vayda raced down the steps and into his arms. He held her with his free arm as she sobbed.

"Are you all right?" Pavielle asked her. His forehead wrinkled with concern.

Vayda nodded and wiped her eyes. "Gangsta's badly hurt, I called 911 already."

"Where is he?" Gouch asked worried.

"In the house inside of the closet," She told him.

"Y'all put them thangs up, if she called the 911. They should be here any minute now, especially with that explosion." Pavielle stated. He handed his weapon over to Gouch and he stashed all of their weapons inside of the trunk.

He tossed the car keys back to Pavielle before he and Killa Dre ran into the ruined house.

Ambulances and police cars had just pulled upon Pavielle and Vayda. Pavielle looked beyond them and saw more police cars headed their way. He watched as the police passed them up and headed to where the smoke was rising in the air in the distance. He looked into the sky and saw a news helicopter heading into the same direction.

"It was me that set off that explosion; I think it blew up whatever car Paybacc left here in." Vayda stood beside her man staring up at the sky.

"What kind of car was he driving in? And what color was it?" Pavielle questioned.

"One of those new Chrysler, it was black on black." Vayda answered.

"I'll be right back." Pavielle hopped into his whip and resurrected the engine. He pulled off heading into the direction the fire was coming from. Reaching his destination, he saw that it was surrounded by police cars. An ambulance and a coroners van were also present. By- standers stood behind police barricades watching the coroners at work. Pavielle hopped out of his whip and ran over to one of the barricades. His eyes peered through the smoke trying to see if he saw a Chrysler 300 that had been wrecked by an explosion. He didn't see one. He saw something under a white sheet. He looked around to see if any of the police officers were watching him and they weren't. They were all occupied with keeping the bystanders at bay.

Pavielle hopped the barricade and ran over to whatever was hid under the white sheet. He drew the sheet back and exposed a body burned to a crisp. Upon further inspection, it dawned on him that it wasn't Paybacc. The person at his feet was much smaller in frame. Pavielle looked beside the body and there was the remains of a bicycle which was also burned back.

"Fuck!" Pavielle cursed and let the sheet fall back over the burned body.

"Aye, get your ass back over the barricade! This is police business!" an officer shouted and pointed at Pavielle.

The young kingpin hopped back over the barricade and disappeared into the crowd of bystanders.

Flashback

Paybacc laughed as he pushed his Chrysler 300 through the streets, guiding it with one hand and using the other to take a band out of the briefcase. He thumbed through the bills, watching the corners of the money move like a stop motion comic book.

Boof! Sssssssss!

"Fuck!" Paybacc cursed hating to hear that familiar sound. He'd just blown out his tire. Paybacc pulled over to the curb and hopped out to check the damage of his tire. A man on a bicycle had just stopped on the sidewalk. He eyeballed the briefcase in the passenger seat of Paybacc's whip. When he saw him kneel to inspect the tire he made his move.

Paybacc stood up to retrieve the spare tire from his trunk when he spotted the man riding off with a brief case. His forehead wrinkled. He ran to the driver's window and his briefcase was gone from the front passenger seat. Angry, he slammed his fist against the roof of his vehicle and snatched his Tec-9 from its hiding place. He ran after the man on the bicycle, firing at him. Winded, Paybacc stopped running and lowered his Tec-9 to his side. Hunched over, he looked on as the man rode off on his bicycle carrying the million dollars that rightfully belonged to him. Suddenly, the man exploded and sent burning Benjamin Franklins into the air, along with a cloud of smoke. The explosion was so loud that it set off the car alarms of near by parked cars and imploded their windows. Paybacc couldn't believe what he'd just witnessed. He ran back to his car, tossed his Tec-9 inside and popped the trunk. He removed the spare tire and quickly changed his flat.

Present

Pavielle, Gouch, Killa Dre, Vayda, Black Jesus, Bullet and Creeper were all sitting inside of the waiting room at UCLA hospital. Everyone wore grim expressions as they impatiently waited for the doctor's verdict. A tall, slender white man in a lab coat stepped into the waiting room stealing everyone's attention from their thoughts. Pavielle rose from his seat and approached him. Everyone was on the edge of their seats hoping that Gangsta would be all right. Once the doctor left, Pavielle closed his eyes and hung his head. In a fit, he punched the wall and sobbed, allowing tears to cascade down his face. A weeping Vayda rose from her seat and comforted him. Gouch buried his face into the palms of his hands. A glassy eyed Killa Dre gripped his shoulder trying to console him. Black Jesus and Bullet hung their heads, while Creeper tilted his head back against the wall and closed his eyes. Everyone was devasted by the lost of Gangsta. He had impacted everyone's life in the waiting room in one way or another. Without him they knew that life would never be the same.

Chapter Seventeen

Months Later

Vayda lay in bed with her hair in a mess and her face glistening from perspiration. She wore a loving smile as she stared down at her bundle of joy. She'd just given birth to a healthy baby boy. Pavielle stood beside her bed wearing a smile as he peered down at his son.

"Wow, babe, we created this lil' man, he's beautiful." Vayda said of their baby boy.

Pavielle kissed Vayda affectionately. "What do you wanna name him?"

Vayda thought on it for a moment, then said, "Nasheed Charles Hood; after the two men that died protecting his life." She looked to her fiancé for his input.

Pavielle nodded, "OK."

He scooped the little Nasheed into his arms and walked around the room, cradling his seed. He talked in a tone that only him and he could hear. Little Nasheed was a mirror resemblance of his father, except he had a scalp full of dark curly hair and grey eyes. Pavielle didn't know exactly who he'd inherited his eyes from, but he assumed it must have been from Vayda's side of the family since he didn't know of any relatives of his that had grey eyes.

Pavielle looked to the doorway; Gouch and Killa Dre were just stepping inside. They both wore smiles.

"Is that my nephew?" Gouch asked excitedly as he approached. Pavielle nodded and allowed his brother to take his little nephew into his arms. "Hey, man. What's up? I'm your uncle Gucci. Welcome to the world, blood drop. Booby, this lil' nigga looks just like you, that's brazy."

Gouch continued talking to little Nasheed while Vayda and Pavielle looked on. Pavielle looked over to Killa Dre who was standing beside Gouch admiring his son. The young kingpin whispered something to his lady and she nodded.

"Let Dre hold'em, Gucci." Pavielle told his big brother. Gouch handed the baby over to Killa Dre. The young nigga beamed as he held the baby in his arms. Pavielle gripped the young boy's shoulder and said, "Killa, me and Vay would like you to be lil' man's Godfather, what do you say?"

Killa Dre smiled proudly and said, "Alright."

"We're gonna set it up and make it official." Pavielle told him. "But listen, if anything was to ever happen to me, you gotta take care of lil' dude like he came out of your nut sack. Do you understand, Blood?" Killa Dre looked into Pavielle's eyes wearing a dead serious expression and nodded yes. "Alright," Pavielle patted him on the shoulder.

Pavielle, Gouch and Killa Dre chilled out in the cafeteria chopping it up. The night was dark and cold, so when ever they spoke they could see their white breath.

"This is a new beginning for me; I gotta fiancé and a seed now. That means I gotta get rid everything out there in this fucked up world that poses a threat to them, you Griff me? We gotta put the smash on Paybacc, Blood. Until that mothafucka is six feet under, this world ain't safe for either of us." Gouch and Killa Dre nodded in understanding. "Are y'all with me?"

"Blood, you ain't even gotta ask." Killa Dre slapped hands with Pavielle and embraced him.

"We're brothas, nigga; you already know what it is." Gouch embraced his little brother.

Together the collective would be a force to be reckoned with.

The next day

Beth sat behind the plexiglass impatiently waiting for her husband to come out for his visit. Arsenegger was charged with double homicide and sentenced to life without the possibility of parole. He'd been locked up at Corcoran state penitentiary for the past three months. He'd been doing his time in protective custody for a time, but after a month in he requested to be moved into general population. He knew that it was probably a bad idea given that he was an ex homicide detective and all. But he couldn't do the remainder of his time in P.C. Twenty-three hours on lock down with only his thoughts to keep him company was starting to drive him bat shit crazy. So he decided to throw caution to the wind and take his chances in general population.

A smile emerged on Beth's face when she saw her husband walking towards her draped in his prison uniform. His face was shaved cleaned and he'd grown his hair out. He now rocked it past his shoulders. He beamed brightly when he locked eyes with Beth and sat down on the tiny stool. He picked up the telephone and pressed it to his ear.

"Hey, beautiful," Arsenegger addressed his wife with a loving smile.

"Hey, there, hubby," Beth replied, happy to see her man.

"Where's my little princess?"

"My mother's watching her; I think she's coming down with the flu. I'll be sure to bring her on my next visit."

"OK. But don't bring her if she's still under the weather. How is everything at home?"

"Everything is just peachy. You've left plenty of money to take care of me and Tonai. Though I have to admit that it isn't much of a home without you there," Her eyes became glassy and displayed her hurt over his incarceration.

"I know, sweetheart, and I'm sorry. But there's nothing I can do about it. I made my bed, and now I have to lie in it."

Beth wiped her tearing eyes. "So, how are you doing? Are you making it all right in here? I mean, does anyone know that you used to be a..."

"No one knows a thing. I've been getting by in here just fine. I ran into a couple of knuckleheads when I first got in, and I made an example out of them. After a few guys saw what I did to them, I was given a wide berth. Don't you worry about me, I can hold my own."

Beth closed her eyes and blew hard. She opened them and said, "Thank God. I've been really worried about you in here."

"Aye, look at me," Arsenegger knocked on the plexiglass for his wife's attention. "This is a school of gladiators, and only the strong will survive." He stared Beth in the eyes. "Only the strong will survive."

Arsenegger and Beth went on with their conversation until his visit was over. He placed his palm flat on the plexiglass and his wife placed hers on top of his from the opposite side. She mouthed "I love you" and he mouthed it back.

After the visit

Arsenegger stood before the small mirror in his cell's smearing cherry Kool Aide on his lips. His hair was parted down the middle and he wore it in two pigtails. He was in a wife-beater that he wore tied into a knot above his navel. A muscular, bald head brother approached him from behind and hugged him lovingly, kissing on the side of his neck and nibbling on his earlobe. Arsenegger closed his eyes trying to fight back the urge to vomit. He was repulsed by the thought of another man touching him. The bald brother turned Arsenegger around to face him and caressed his cheek. Arsenegger took his hand and sucked on his middle-finger, staring him square in his eyes. This caused the brother to smile and his dick to get as hard as steel prison bars. He pulled his meat out from the opening in his boxers and lowered Arsenegger to his knees by gently pushing his head downward. Down on his knees and face to face with a rock hard dick, Arsenegger closed his eyes to fight back the tears. He repeated what he'd told his wife "only the strong survive" before taking the hard black cock into his mouth.

$$$

Chingo was hunched over a glass table before three lines of cocaine. He had a rolled up $100 dollar bill and was snorting the white lines through it. Beside him there were a box of sandwich bags, a digital scale, two playing cards and a black Glock .9mm. Chingo was a mixture of Mexican and African American. He had the complexion of a dark skinned Latino and the features of a black man. He rocked twisties and a shallow goatee. Black shades sat at the top of Chingo's head. He had a top row of gold teeth which spelled out his name. Homeboy was about making money, and he was not above murdering anyone that was in the way of him doing so.

After taking a line into his right nostril, Chingo lifted his head up and wiped his nose. Seeing the reflection of someone behind him in the glass table, he grabbed his Glock .9mm and whipped around. He was just about to squeeze the trigger when his visitor's face registered inside of his head. Sighing with relief, he lowered his gun and continued to wipe his nose.

"Cuz, you scared the shit outta me." Chingo told his uninvited guest.

"I thought I would have seen you at Domino's service."

"I had a few moves to make. The homie will forgive me, he knew my heart. I dropped by the repass though, and dropped a few bands on his mom's." Chingo went along snorting another line. His guest sat at the opposite end of the glass table. He leaned back in his chair and propped his boots upon the table, nestling his hands in his lap. Chingo noticed the specs of blood at the toes of his boots. "What's up with that?" he nodded to the red stains on the man's boots.

"Couple of youngins didn't wanna pay their taxes; they weren't familiar with me and my sins so I had to bring them up to speed." The man winced. He pulled a revolver from his waistline and sat it down on the glass table. It had been digging into his hip.

Chingo looked from the revolver then up into his guest's eyes, scowling. "Cuz, I know you didn't come here to put the strong arm on me for no taxes. You already know that under The Three Headed Monster I operated under immunity for all that I've done for the set. So, if you think you're 'bout to put the muscle on me for some paper, we can grab our hammers and get to it. Notta drop of bitch pollutes this bloodline." He spoke the truth from between those gold teeth of his. He may have been a lot of things but he for damn sure wasn't no punk ass nigga.

"Be easy, Loco. I'm not here for that." He held up his hands to let Chingo know he came in peace. "I just came by to see if you were going to be with me when I go to pay a call upon Mr. Booby Loco. I'm recruiting a pack of hungry young wolves for this special mission, and I want chu to be the pick of the litter."

Chingo's nodded and said, "I'm with chu, cuzzo. I fucked with Domino and Nightmare, and Wacko was the homie; a trill nigga fa' sho'." He pounded his fist to his chest.

The man smirked and nodded. "Good."

He walked over to Chingo's end of the table and picked up the rolled up $100 dollar bill. He snorted a line, leant his head back, and pinched his nose shut so he wouldn't sneeze. Feeling the effects of the powdered substance, his eyes rolled to their whites and his body shook. "That's some decent coke, who's your connect, cuz?" He flicked and wiped his nose.

"What's it to you, Paybacc?"

Elsewhere

Porno lay back on his plush black leather couch smoking a fat ass Kush blunt while a slim blonde's head bobbed up and down his dick. Slurping sounds bounced off the walls of the living room. While the Becky handled her business, Porno read over an old news paper clipping. Its headline read: Dirty detective sentenced to life in prison. There was a picture of Arsenegger inside the court room standing before a judge. Porno smiled victoriously.

To Be Continued...

Me and My Hittas 5

AVAILABLE NOW BY TRANAY ADAMS

The Devil Wears Timbs 1-7

Bury Me A G 1-5

These Scandalous Streets 1-3

A South Central Love Affair

Me and My Hittas 1-6

The Last Real Nigga Alive 1-3

God Bless the Trappers 1-3

A Gangsta's Empire 1-4

Fangeance

Fear My Gangsta 1-5

A Hood Nigga's Blues

The Realest Killaz 1-3

The Last of the OGs 1-3

The Streets Don't Love Nobody 1-2

The Dopeman's Bodyguard 1-2

King of the Trenches